April
Upstairs

ALSO BY SUSAN BETH PFEFFER

Darcy Downstairs

APRIL UPSTAIRS

Susan Beth Pfeffer

HENRY HOLT AND COMPANY
New York

First Edition
Published by Henry Holt and Company, Inc.,
115 West 18th Street, New York, New York 10011.
Published in Canada by Fitzhenry & Whiteside Limited,
195 Allstate Parkway, Markham, Ontario L3R 4T8.

Library of Congress Cataloging-in-Publication Data
Pfeffer, Susan Beth.
April upstairs / Susan Beth Pfeffer.
Summary: Twelve-year-old April has trouble making friends at her
new middle school, until her father's friendship with a missing rock
star catapults her into the news and suddenly makes her popular.
ISBN 0-8050-1306-7 (alk. paper)
[1. Friendship—Fiction.   2. Popularity—Fiction.]   I. Title.
PZ7.P44855Ap   1990
[Fic]—dc20   90-44022

Henry Holt books are available at special discounts
for bulk purchases for sales promotions, premiums,
fund-raising, or educational use. Special editions
or book excerpts can also be created to specification.

Designed by Katy Riegel
Printed in the United States of America
on acid-free paper.

1 2 3 4 5 6 7 8 9 10

To Joel
    Cynthia
    Rachel and
    Sarah Weintraub

APRIL
UPSTAIRS

ONE

*A*pril! April, where are you?"

"In my room," April Hughes called back. Her voice was muffled because her skirt was currently over her head, but she suspected by the time it reached its proper location, her cousin Darcy would find her.

Sure enough, in popped Darcy. "Are you ready?" she asked. "I am. I've been up for ages. Is that what you're wearing?"

"I thought you said you liked it," April said. She tucked her blouse in and began to worry. The new school she was attending, Fairfield Academy, had a dress code—no slacks for girls unless the temperature was below freezing—but even so, it felt weird putting on a skirt. Of course, it was the first day of school. Even Darcy, who always wore slacks, had a skirt on.

"I do, I guess," Darcy replied. "It looked different yesterday."

"I had a different blouse on," April said. "Don't you like this one?" Ordinarily she wouldn't have cared what Darcy thought about her clothes, but this was a first day at a new school, and Darcy somehow represented all the strange girls April would have to meet.

Darcy examined her cousin carefully. "Great choice of blouses," she said, with what was for her a momentous effort at tact. "Terrific just-about-matching skirt. You're going to be the prettiest girl at Fairfield, and the best dressed."

April giggled. What she loved best about Darcy was her inability to be simple. "All I want is not to look stupid," she said.

"You won't," Darcy replied. "I guess you must be nervous."

"Aren't you?" April asked.

"Just 'cause it's the first day of school?" Darcy said. "Nah. This is my second year at the Middle School, after all. I know what I'm in for."

"How's Isabelle doing?" April asked, checking herself one more time in the mirror. She'd begged her mother to let her get her ears pierced, but her mother had insisted she hold off until she was officially a teenager, and that wasn't for another eight months. April knew that with earrings her outfit, and she, would look perfect.

"She's writing a poem," Darcy replied. "An ode

2

to the first day of school." She plopped herself on April's bed. "She's driving Mom crazy. Mom keeps calling her to breakfast, and Isabelle keeps saying, 'You can't interrupt the muse.' We had pancakes, too, because it's the first day. Mom always goes in for those traditional kinds of things on first days and birthdays." She paused for a moment. "Hey, that's a poem," she said. "First days. Birthdays. And I didn't even need a muse."

"April! Are you ready?"

"Just about, Mom," April said. "Darcy, are you sure I'm okay?"

"You're beautiful," Darcy declared. "And I should know. Don't I have the keenest visual eye in this household?"

April laughed. Darcy's parents—April's aunt and uncle—owned Video To Go, the local video store. They loved old movies and were forever bringing them home from the store. Darcy loved them too, and she constantly noticed things none of the others did, so Uncle Bill, Darcy's father, was constantly going on about her keen visual eye. Isabelle, who was almost sixteen and determined to be a poet, claimed she couldn't be bothered to look, but April suspected she was a little jealous of Darcy's ability to see and remember. April was, or at least of the fuss everyone made over Darcy.

"Oh, hi, Darcy," April's mother, Joanne, said as she walked into her daughter's bedroom. "I thought I heard voices in here."

"Mom, why can't I get my ears pierced?" April asked. "Right now, before school starts."

"And who do you think is going to pierce them for you?" Joanne asked. "Ear piercers almost never make emergency house calls."

"You could," April said. "You're a nurse. Nurses pierce ears all the time."

"I'm a nurse practitioner," Joanne replied. "And nurse practitioners are specifically forbidden to pierce their daughters' ears. It's in the oath I took. Do you have all your things together? We only have a few more minutes."

"I'm all ready," Darcy said. "All my stuff is downstairs."

"Then maybe you should go downstairs," Joanne said. "We'll meet you on the front porch in five minutes."

But before Darcy had a chance to get up, the doorbell rang. "Ours or yours?" Joanne asked.

"Yours," Darcy replied. "Trust my keen ears."

"I'll get it," April said.

"I'll go with you," Darcy said. The two girls ran through April's apartment, down the flight of stairs, and to the front door, which was shared by both apartments—April's upstairs, and Darcy's downstairs. April opened the door.

"Flowers for Ms. April Hughes," the man said.

"That's me!" April said.

The florist handed her a giant flower arrangement, grinned, and left. April located the card, and read it. " 'Here's a wonderful start to a wonderful year. Love, Dad.' Oh, Darcy, he remembered! He sent me flowers all the way from Nairobi."

Upstairs and downstairs doors opened, and April found herself and her flowers being looked at by all the members of her family, her mother looking down, her aunt Karen and uncle Bill and cousin Isabelle on the first floor.

"They look like American flowers to me," Isabelle declared.

"He probably called New York and asked them to make the arrangements," Joanne called from upstairs. "April, bring them up now. You can admire them after school."

"Can I take the card with me?" April asked.

Joanne nodded. "Slip it into your bag," she said. "But hurry. We haven't got all day."

April no longer worried about her outfit, no longer minded her unpierced ears. Her father, whom she hadn't seen in three months and probably wouldn't see for another three, had remembered just when the first day of school was, called his network office in New York, and told them to send her flowers. Suddenly having a father stuck in Kenya seemed like a wonderful thing to her.

"I'll meet you in a minute," Darcy said. "I wish my father sent me flowers."

"I will when you win your first Oscar," her father said. "Come on, Darce. You too, Isabelle. Forget the muse for a moment and get ready."

April ran upstairs, clutching the flower arrangement. "Can I keep it in my room?" she asked her mother.

"They're your flowers—keep them wherever you want," her mother replied. "Sorry. That sounded mean, didn't it? It's just we're in a hurry, and I wish your father had sent the flowers yesterday."

"They wouldn't have been so special then," April said.

Her mother sighed. "I know," she said. "Not as special, but definitely easier. Come on. You have everything now?"

"I guess so," April said, and all of a sudden she felt nervous again. She ran to the mirror, checked her outfit, grabbed her bag, and followed her mother downstairs.

Karen peeked her head out as April and Joanne reached the front door. "Darcy's ready," she said. "She's waiting for you by the car."

Joanne smiled at her sister. "First day," she said. "Always a big one."

Karen smiled back. "They'll do fine," she said. "I'll see you this evening. Good luck, April, with all the new girls."

"Thanks, Aunt Karen," April said. She opened her bag and felt for her father's card. Its crisp edges rubbed comfortingly against her fingers.

"Darcy gets dropped off first," Joanne said as though they didn't know, as though they hadn't gone over the arrangements for first day of school a hundred times over the past week. "You might as well get in the front seat, honey, next to me."

April climbed into the backseat first, pushed the passenger seat upright, and watched as Darcy got in. Joanne checked that they all had their seat belts on, then started the car.

"I can't wait for school to start," Darcy said. "I think I'm going to run for student council. Does Fairfield have a student council?"

"I don't know," April said.

"I'm sure it must," her mother said. "They may not call it that, but just about every school has one."

"Then you could run for your student council too," Darcy said. "We could campaign together."

"We go to different schools," April said.

"That's why it would be so great," Darcy replied. "I bet nobody's ever done that, campaigned at a school she doesn't go to."

"I don't think so," April said. She wished Darcy would stop chattering. It only made her stomach hurt worse.

But Darcy didn't seem to notice. "Actually, I think I'll run for an office this year instead," she said. "Treasurer of the student council. I love money. Sometimes I think I should be a great film producer instead of a great film director, so I can control all that money."

"You could be a producer-director," Joanne said.

7

April had noticed that her mother never laughed at any of Darcy's ambitions. Not that she laughed at April's either. But she found reasons why they might not work out. If Darcy said she wanted to be queen of England, April's mother would just say it was a great idea.

"Darcy Greene, producer-director," Darcy said. "I like that. I like the way it sounds. Thanks, Aunt Joanne."

"Any time," Joanne said. "Just remember me in your Oscar speech."

"Which one?" Darcy asked. "I'm going to win hundreds of them."

"The first one then," Joanne said. "Before you get bored and jaded."

Darcy turned around and faced April. "I'll mention you, too," she said. "Or do you want to star in my movie?"

April blushed. Her mother didn't know she sometimes dreamed about being an actress. "Let me get through seventh grade first," she said. "Then I'll decide."

"Okay," Darcy said. "I guess when I'm a great film director, people'll send me flowers all the time."

"You'll be sick and tired of them after a while," Joanne declared. "Flowers morning, noon, and night."

"I can always give them to the poor," Darcy replied. "I have to do stuff like that to become a humanitarian."

"Oh, that's right," Joanne said. "I'd forgotten you planned to be one of those, as well."

April stared out the window. She and her mother had moved to the town of West Devon two months ago. Before then, they'd lived in Oakcrest, about a hundred miles away. April had gone to two schools there, Russell Elementary and Oakcrest Middle School. Before Oakcrest, they'd lived in Newton for a year, while her mother got her nurse practitioner's degree, and before that they'd lived in Madrid, Spain. April wondered if any of the other girls at Fairfield had gone to school in Madrid. She'd only been there for two years, and by the end of the two years her parents had fought all the time and wound up getting divorced, with her father moving to Nairobi and she and her mother moving back to the States. Since then, she got to see her father only a couple of times a year. She missed him all the time, but especially on days like today.

Darcy's parents, Aunt Karen and Uncle Bill, had stayed married. Sometimes they fought, and April could hear them through the floor of their apartment. But they never fought the angry way her parents had, and when April had asked once if Darcy worried they might get divorced, Darcy had only laughed. Maybe that was why April's mother leaped at the chance to buy the top floor of the

9

two-family house Darcy's family lived in, so April could at least have an uncle nearby, if not a father. And April could see how close her mother was to her sister Karen.

The two families kept separate apartments and fairly separate lives, but with Darcy and April the same age, it was inevitable their homes would flow into each other's. Darcy slept over in April's room a couple of nights a week, and April and her mother were always having supper with Darcy's family. It was different from what April was used to (just her and her mother, no noise, no confusion) but she had to admit she enjoyed it.

"Whoops, there's my school," Darcy said. "Thanks, Aunt Joanne. Have a great day, April. I'll see you later." She hardly waited for Joanne to park the car before she flew out and down the main walk to the school building. April watched as first one, then two, then five or more kids spotted Darcy, and walked or even ran to her side. By the time Darcy was at the front steps, she was surrounded by a dozen boys and girls.

"You'll make friends soon too," April's mother said to April.

But April knew it would be different. Darcy was popular. April could tell that from the way the phone always rang, the kids who were forever dropping by. Darcy made every effort to have April included in her plans, but April knew she'd be going to a different school and would have to make friends on her own. And April could never remember a time in any of her different schools when she had more than two or three really good friends.

"Do you want me to go in with you?" her mother asked as she turned left and started down the street toward Fairfield.

"No, thanks," April said. "I can do it myself."

"I know you can," her mother said. "The question is, do you want to?"

All April wanted was to go back home, sit in her bedroom, and admire her flowers. "I'll go in by myself," she said. "It might seem kind of babyish to have you come with me. And I don't want to seem babyish on the first day of school."

"There'll be other new girls there," her mother said. "You won't be the only one."

"I know," April said. She wondered if all the new girls felt the way she did, scared and just a little unhappy. She'd liked going to her old middle school. When she'd started there a year before, it hadn't felt like a new school, because she'd known so many of the kids. Not that she would have run for student council. But then again, Darcy liked being in charge. That was why she wanted to be a great film director, so she could boss people around. April just wanted to be left alone.

"I went to a new school once," her mother said. "Well, more than once, of course, but once when we moved. I was in fifth grade, and Karen was in eighth. I was never so scared in my life. My mother walked in with me, and boy, was I glad. She held my hand and everything. Nobody thought I was babyish."

"I'm in seventh grade, Mom," April pointed out.

"That's right," her mother said. "How could I have forgotten?" She slowed down the car as they approached the school grounds. Fairfield looked different from Darcy's middle school—less friendly, more imposing. April saw the school grounds covered with girls of all ages. They all had skirts and blouses on, except for a few in dresses. She'd dressed all right, even though she was sure she'd be the only girl in seventh grade without pierced ears.

"Last chance for an escort," her mother said.

"Just drop me off here," April said. She searched around in her bag once again, found her father's card, and let it comfort her. When the car came to a full stop, April took a deep breath, unlocked the door, and let herself out. "Bye, Mom," she said. "See you tonight."

"Bye, love," her mother said.

April began the lonely walk to her new school. Somehow it didn't bother her that her mother stayed in the car, watching the entire time. That was something mothers did, and right then April was glad her mother knew the rules too.

WO

*I*t really wasn't that scary a school once you got inside it, April decided almost immediately, and the girls in it weren't that intimidating either. She found if she looked at everyone's earlobes, to determine if they had pierced ears, she could manage pretty well. Half did, half didn't, and that made her feel better too.

Fairfield was a small school, girls only, and it felt strange at first not to see any boys in her classes. But her parents had picked it because it stressed foreign languages, and April's father believed everybody should be multilingual. Of course, he spoke four different languages besides English, so that was easy enough for him to say (in French, Spanish, Arabic, and Swahili). April, who already spoke Spanish, was scheduled to take French as well. She knew Fairfield would be academically challenging; she just hoped it wouldn't be socially challenging as well.

The first day was a maze of classes, hallways, and strange faces, and a perpetually lost feeling. It didn't help that almost all the other girls knew exactly where they were going and who they were going with. April felt as though NEW GIRL had been tattooed across her forehead. Nobody was rude to her, some girls even smiled or said hi, but she knew she didn't belong, and that hurt. She wished she was back home, any home. She wished she had Darcy with her. She wished her parents had never gotten divorced.

Lunchtime was the worst. Everybody seemed to have somebody to sit with, except April, who sat at the end of a table all by herself. She knew all the things she was supposed to do—introduce herself, smile, ask people's names, look like someone they'd want to be friends with—but she was too miserable and tired. And everybody else was excited and laughing, and to get their attention she'd have to interrupt. April was afraid that if she interrupted, they wouldn't like her. It was better to be quiet.

But toward the end of the lunch period one of the older girls stood up in front of the room, and the other girls quieted down.

"I have announcements," the girl declared, and suddenly April's silence felt natural and called for.

"All girls trying out for the choir should meet

this afternoon in the auditorium. Be prepared to sing."

The girls laughed. April laughed too, and felt some of the tension escape from her body.

"Track-and-field tryouts will be tomorrow after school. Field hockey also meets then. The tennis club will have its first meeting on Thursday."

April tried picturing herself doing each of those activities, but none of them felt right to her. Maybe if the school had an ice-skating club, she'd join it in the winter.

"The *Fairfield Forward*—that's the school magazine, in case you've forgotten—will have its first meeting after school today, in room 112. All girls who have not previously worked on the *Forward* and are interested in doing so should attend the meeting."

That was it. April knew it as soon as she heard. Forget field hockey and singing. She'd write for the *Forward*, make a name for herself that way. It might not be as glamorous as running for student council, but as far as she was concerned, it would be a lot more fun.

She could hardly wait for the school day to end, and her impatience made everything less intimidating. It didn't hurt that her school day ended with Spanish and social studies, her two best subjects. She could see how impressed the other girls were with her Spanish, and that made her feel even better, since she was in a class with girls much older than she. Those two years in Madrid, and her parents' insistence that she not forget everything she'd learned there, really paid off.

The final bell rang, and April glanced down at her notebook for the hundredth time to make sure the room she was supposed to go to really was 112. She hated the idea of ending up in the wrong room, being forced to sing or play field hockey because of simple carelessness. Even finding room 112 seemed less daunting to her, now that she'd spent a day being lost in the school building.

When she got to room 112, there were already a half dozen girls sitting behind desks. A very important-looking girl stood in the front of the room, and a teacher sat beside her.

"Fill out this form, please," the important girl said to April as she walked in. So April took the form, found a desk to sit at, and filled it out. The form wasn't much—just name, address, phone number, grade, and experience writing. April knew the answers to all the questions, except for experience writing. She knew she must have some, but she couldn't figure out how to word it.

Another couple of girls entered the room then, and April looked up to see who they were. She was startled to discover they were identical twins. The important girl, who April guessed was a senior, recognized them right away. "Hi, Megan, Melissa," she said.

The girls said hi back. April stared at them. She had seen identical twins dressed identically before, but these girls were the same down to the last earring. April marveled that they could even tell themselves apart.

"All right," the senior said, gathering up all the forms. "I guess we're ready to begin. My name is Brooke Martin, and I'm the editor of the *Fairfield Forward*. For those of you who are new to Fairfield, the *Forward* is a magazine published every month by the students of Fairfield. To write for the magazine, you have to be in the seventh grade or above. The younger girls have their own magazine, and I can see that most of you are seventh graders. The *Forward* has a long tradition of excellence. Last year we took second prize in a national contest for magazines put out by private schools."

A couple of the girls applauded. April wasn't sure whether to applaud or not, and flapped her hands around until she felt like a jerk.

Brooke smiled at the girls. April wondered if she'd ever be like that—cool, powerful, capable of smiling at a room filled with strangers. "The *Forward* needs writers, of course, but that's not all it needs. We need editors, photographers, layout artists, even girls to distribute the magazine to the different classrooms. So I want you all to give some thought as to the job that most interests you. Every job is important."

A girl's hand shot up. April recognized her from

having been in most of her classes that day. "What if you know you want to be a writer?" the girl asked. "Can you just be one?"

"Most of the girls who work on the *Forward* want to write for it," Brooke replied. "So that's the most competitive area. I'm sorry, I don't know your name."

"Emily," the girl said.

Brooke smiled. "Emily," she said. "We usually don't start seventh graders as writers, but there are exceptions. If you think you really deserve to be a writer, and you can prove it, then that's what you'll be. But even if you don't get to write this year, or next, that doesn't mean you won't have a great time on the *Forward*, or won't be a writer someday. I wrote my first piece for the *Forward*, at least my first that got published, when I was in ninth grade, but by then I'd realized how much I loved editing. All of you might find that too, that the different jobs involved in putting out the magazine interest you more than writing. So don't be discouraged if you don't get to write stories and articles right away."

April immediately felt discouraged.

"Why don't I go around the room and ask each of you what you want to do," Brooke said. "Let's start with you, Emily."

"I want to write," Emily admitted. "I write poems all the time."

"The *Forward* publishes poetry and fiction,"

Brooke said. "As well as articles of interest to the girls at school. Megan, Melissa?"

April almost expected the twins to speak in unison. But they took turns.

"I want to be a photographer," one of them said.

"Me too," the other one said.

Brook laughed. "I was sort of hoping you'd each want something different," she said. "That would be a first for you."

The other girls laughed. April didn't bother. She was starting to get nervous about what she should say when Brooke called on her.

"You, sitting behind Megan," Brooke said. "Or is it Melissa?"

"You mean me?" the girl asked.

Brooke nodded. "Yes, you," she said.

"I don't really know what I want," the girl said. "My mother said I had to do something after school, and I can't sing."

Brooke nodded. "I'm sure we'll find something for you," she said. "You, the girl in the blue-and-gray blouse."

April looked down and realized Brooke had called on her. "My name is April Hughes," she said, in case Brooke wanted to know.

Brooke smiled at her. "Thank you," she said. "I should have been asking for introductions."

April wasn't sure whether it was good she'd done something Brooke wanted her to without Brooke's asking. "April Hughes," she said again. "And I just started here today. I used to go to school someplace else." She knew Brooke hadn't asked for her autobiography, but she'd had it pent up inside her all day long, waiting for someone to ask. "I'm in seventh grade," she continued, "and I want to be a writer." She didn't know until that moment that she really did want to write, and she didn't want to wait, either, not until ninth grade. "I want to write articles," she said, to differentiate herself from Emily and her poetry. "About real people, and things that are going on. I know about that because my father's a foreign correspondent."

"Oh?" Brooke said. "Does he work for a newspaper?"

April shook her head. "He's the African affairs expert for DBC-TV," she replied. "He lives in Kenya."

"Is he African?" Emily asked.

"No. He's from Wisconsin," April said. "He used to be the head of the Spanish bureau, and we lived in Madrid, but then the network had cutbacks and lots of people lost their jobs, and Daddy said he was lucky they were willing to keep him on, even if it did mean moving to Kenya. So he learned Swahili. That's what they speak there."

"What's his name?" Brooke asked. "My parents watch DBC news at six thirty. Maybe I've seen him."

"Mitchell Hughes," April said. "He doesn't get

to be on much. He says lots of interesting things happen in Africa all the time, but Americans don't care enough, so they don't give him much airtime. Mostly wars and famines."

Brooke nodded. "I hate famines," she said. "Whenever they show starving people on TV, I change the channel. It just upsets me too much to look at them."

"Then maybe you've never seen him," April said. "But he's real important anyway."

"That's really interesting," Brooke said. "Is your mother a reporter too?"

"She's a nurse practitioner," April said. "That's like being a nurse, only better. She had to get an extra degree. We just moved to West Devon a couple of months ago. I guess I know a lot about health, too, but I really think I should write articles on important stuff like world affairs."

"The *Fairfield Forward* doesn't publish much on world affairs," Brooke said, and April thought she saw the teacher-advisor stifle a laugh. April hated herself for being such a fool, going on about her parents when none of the other girls had. She was sure they were all laughing at her, and she blushed.

"All right," Brooke said. "You, sitting next to April."

"I wanted to write articles too," the girl said. "But I guess I'm not as qualified as she is."

"Who, me?" April asked.

The girl nodded. "My father's just a surgeon,"

she said. "And my mother doesn't do anything except work on committees and play golf. I didn't even know where that country was, the one April's father lives in, with all the wars and famines and everything."

"All right," Brooke said. "I think I should make one thing clear. You don't have to know where Kenya is to write for the *Fairfield Forward*. The magazine publishes lots of different kinds of things, but we do aim for material that all the girls at school will find interesting. We're not *Newsweek*. Nobody expects us to cover foreign affairs."

April didn't know her cheeks could get that red. She would have run out of the room if she could, but instead she sat absolutely still and vowed never to say another word again. Maybe it wasn't too late to register at West Devon Middle School. Or maybe she could move to Kenya and live with her father and learn Swahili. In Kenya, nobody would expect her to talk.

The teacher stood up then. "I'm Mrs. Holcomb," she said. "And what I think Brooke is trying to say is there's room at the *Forward* for girls with all different interests. I, for one, think an article or two on world events might be interesting, if we could find a specific Fairfield slant. And you, whose mother plays golf, perhaps you could contribute a piece about Fairfield's golf team. We came in third in the state championship last year, you know." Mrs. Holcomb smiled, and April felt a lot better. "I probably shouldn't have interrupted," she said. "But I did want each and every one of you to feel welcome."

Brooke nodded. "I did too," she said. "I mean, I want that too. All right. There are still a couple of you who haven't told us what you're interested in."

April hardly listened to their replies. She knew she'd spoken too much, and she wished she hadn't, but things didn't seem nearly as bad as they had just moments before. She began concentrating again when Mrs. Holcomb spoke, telling the girls about the history of the *Fairfield Forward,* and when Brooke passed around copies of last year's issues, April seized hers eagerly. It was a great-looking magazine, complete with photographs, drawings, articles, poems, and fiction. She bet it was better than anything the West Devon Middle School might put out, and then she felt funny, being so competitive, when twenty minutes earlier all she'd wanted was to leave Fairfield and never see it again.

April felt so much better about things that when Brooke called an end to the meeting, she hung around to talk to her and Mrs. Holcomb. The other girls filed out of the room, but April deliberately lingered.

"I just wanted to apologize," she said, although that wasn't what she really wanted at all. "Talking about my family that way. I just got overexcited. It's my first day here, and I knew I should have stopped, but my mouth wouldn't let me."

Mrs. Holcomb grinned. "I have a mouth like that myself sometimes," she said.

"I hope you'll give me a chance to write," April continued. "Not because of my father or anything. I mean, I don't know that much about Africa myself, and I don't think I could come up with a Fairfield slant. Not until I've been here for a while, and I've gotten to know all the slants, if you know what I mean. But I think I'm a good writer, and I'd really like the chance to try."

"I told you the writing competition is quite stiff," Brooke said. "I can't guarantee anything."

"I understand," April replied. "But I'd still like the chance."

"Why don't you submit a piece?" Mrs. Holcomb said. "When you think you've written something of interest to all of us. Then if Brooke, and the rest of the editorial staff, think you have talent, you can keep right on writing."

"Thank you," April said. "I'll do that."

"But don't expect too much," Brooke said. "Not right away."

"I won't," April said, but already her mind was busy with article ideas. "Thank you."

"Thank you," Mrs. Holcomb said. "It's nice to see such enthusiasm."

April smiled as she left the classroom. She hadn't expected her first friend at Fairfield to be a teacher, but she didn't care. Where there was one friend, others were sure to follow.

THREE

*M*y life's in a rut," April complained to Darcy
a week later. They were sitting in April's room,
April on a chair, and Darcy crosslegged on April's
bed. The only thing that separated Darcy's room
from her sister Isabelle's was a plywood partition
their father had erected for them, and Darcy preferred visiting April to having April visit her.

"How can your life be in a rut?" Darcy asked.
"You just started a new school a week ago. You
only moved here a couple of months ago. How
could a rut set in that fast?"

April had the uncomfortable feeling Darcy's life
was perpetually rut free. "I know everything's new
and different," she said. "But I still don't have any
friends. And I haven't been able to come up with a
single idea for an article for the *Forward*."

"You could interview me," Darcy said.

"I don't think that would have a Fairfield slant," April replied. "The only things you know about Fairfield are what I've told you."

"That's not true," Darcy said. "There's a girl in Isabelle's class who went to Fairfield for a couple of years, then transferred to the high school. She told Isabelle all about Fairfield, and Isabelle told me."

"Yeah?" April asked. "What did she say?"

"Nothing interesting," Darcy admitted. "Just that classes were small, and there weren't any boys. She liked boys a lot. Isabelle says she made up for two years of not having any in about two weeks' time."

"I don't think that's enough of a Fairfield slant," April said. "I think I'm going to be in a rut forever."

"Why don't you do something about it?" Darcy asked, sounding horribly like April's mother.

"Do what?" April asked. If Darcy suggested getting out of her rut by cleaning her room, April would scream.

"Make friends," Darcy said. "Then at least you could be in a rut with other people."

"You can't just make friends," April said. "Friendships have to grow like flowers."

"Don't tell Isabelle that," Darcy said. "She'll turn it into a poem."

April giggled. "I didn't mean to be poetic," she said. "It just came out that way."

"Aren't there girls in your class you like?" Darcy asked. "Girls you'd like to be friends with?"

"Sure," April said. "There's Katie. I met her at the *Forward* meeting. Her father's a surgeon and her mother plays golf, but that isn't why I like her."

"Why do you like her?" Darcy asked.

"She's nice," April said. "I've talked with her a couple of times since the *Forward* meeting, and she always smiles when she sees me. I'm hoping she'll ask me to have lunch with her someday."

"Why don't you ask her?" Darcy said.

April shook her head. "She eats lunch with the twins," she replied. "Megan and Melissa. And a couple of other girls. I couldn't just barge in on them."

"Do you like Megan and Melissa?" Darcy asked.

"I'm not sure," April said. "They're kind of intimidating. They dress alike and they look alike, and I'm always scared I'll call Megan Melissa or Melissa Megan, or even worse I'll call both of them Miranda, and then they'll ask me why, and I'll have to tell them I had a cat named Miranda, and that might make them mad at me."

"Do they ever talk to you?" Darcy asked.

"Sometimes," April said. "Yesterday Megan or Melissa asked me if I'd come up with any articles for the *Forward*. I was afraid she was being snotty, but then I could see she really wasn't. She wanted to know. She said she'd want to take pictures for it if I did. She wants to be a news photographer.

Whichever one she is, the other one wants to be a fashion photographer. I don't see how anybody can tell them apart."

"I have twins in my class," Darcy said. "Robert and Rachel."

"It's easier to tell them apart if they're not both girls," April declared. "And even if Rachel came to Fairfield, I wouldn't have any trouble telling her apart from Robert because there are no boys allowed."

"That's right," Darcy said. "Okay. You like Katie and Megan and Melissa, and they all seem to like you too."

"I didn't say that," April replied.

"You said they talked to you," Darcy declared. "That's good enough. Why don't you invite them over?"

"Oh, I couldn't," April said.

"Why not?" Darcy said.

April wanted to tell Darcy the truth, but knew she didn't dare. Katie and Megan and Melissa all lived in beautiful mansions. Not that April had ever seen their houses, but she just knew they had to be mansions. Megan and Melissa were taken to and from school every day by a chauffeur. And Katie's father was a surgeon and her mother didn't even have to work. Meanwhile, April was living in the top half of a two-family house. It was a wonderful house, and a great top half, and April loved having her aunt and uncle and cousins just a staircase away, but it was no mansion. And her mother was a nurse practitioner, which was better than a nurse, but not nearly as important as a surgeon. She shuddered to think what the twins' father did that made him so rich.

But she couldn't tell Darcy any of that, because Darcy would think that Megan and Melissa and Katie were snobs, or maybe worse, that April was one herself. "I don't know them well enough to," she said instead, and the excuse sounded feeble even to her.

"You'll never get to know them unless you work at it," Darcy said. "You think I've always had friends?"

"Yes," April said.

Darcy grinned. "Well, maybe I have," she said. "But lots of times I'll meet someone I think could be a friend, and I don't just sit back and wait for that friendship to happen. I say hello, I join her for lunch, I invite her to my house. And that's how we become friends."

"We're different," April replied. "You can do that kind of thing. I can't."

"Do you want me to do it for you?" Darcy asked.

"No," April said.

"Then you'd better do it for yourself," Darcy declared. "I want you to invite them tomorrow.

Have them come on Thursday. Isabelle has a drama-club meeting, so we'll have the house all to ourselves. That'll impress them."

"Just ask them over?" April said.

Darcy nodded. "People like it when other people like them," she said. "They'll be flattered. You'll see. Start with Katie and Megan and Melissa, and you'll end up with more friends than you'll know what to do with."

April wished she had the courage to refuse, but she knew Darcy would keep pestering her. "I'll try," she said. "But don't be surprised if they say no."

April was the one who was surprised. When she approached Katie, Megan, and Melissa before school the next day, they all agreed to come over Thursday afternoon.

"I've never met a real television star before," Katie said.

"Who?" April asked.

"Your father," Katie replied. "You did say he was a TV star, didn't you?"

April doubted those had been her exact words. "He's a reporter on TV," she said. "And he lives in Kenya. That's in Africa. And even if he didn't live in Africa, my parents are divorced, so he wouldn't live with us, anyway." She waited for Katie to take back her acceptance of the invitation, but she didn't.

"That's probably better," she said instead. "I'd get nervous meeting a real TV star."

"We meet TV stars all the time," one of the twins declared. "Daddy is a big Broadway producer, and TV stars come over to our parties."

"They always say how cute we are," the other twin said. "Sometimes we step on their toes, or we just kind of kick them to see if they'll still say we're cute, and they do."

"They want Daddy to hire them," the first twin said. "So they have to say we're cute."

"But April's father is a reporter," the second twin said. "That means even if he comes home from Kenya, he still won't want Daddy to put him on Broadway. He isn't that kind of TV star."

Twin number one nodded. "So we can be friends with you," she said to April. "If you want, our chauffeur can drive all of us to your home tomorrow."

"That'd be great," April said. She couldn't believe it. Not only had Katie and the twins accepted her invitation, they were talking about being friends, and giving her a chauffeur-driven lift home. She knew she owed Darcy a thousand thank-yous.

But after school that day, all her feelings of jubilation vanished. The house looked shoddy. The grass needed mowing. One of the stained-glass windows in the attic was missing a piece of its stained glass.

April checked her bedroom out thoroughly. It was a pretty room, and ordinarily she loved the way it overlooked the oak-lined street, but she knew Katie and Melissa and Megan would be expecting something more. And they wouldn't be expecting Darcy.

What if they hated her? What if they never talked to anybody who went to public school? What if they were snobs, and they went back to Fairfield the next day and told everybody that April wasn't rich and her father probably wasn't a big TV star after all? Not that April had ever said he was. But as long as the other girls thought it, April felt a little more glamorous.

April ate very little supper that night and even less breakfast the next morning. It didn't seem fair somehow that making new friends should be so impossible. Other girls did it. Darcy did it without even trying. Only April was doomed to a lifetime of solitude, if you could call having Darcy in your bedroom six hours a day solitude.

Still, it was fun having the twins' chauffeur hold the door open for her. Even Katie seemed to enjoy it, but she didn't have a chauffeur either.

"We have a housekeeper," she said as the girls were driven to April's home. "Mrs. Dorman. If it's raining, and Mom's busy, she picks me up after school."

"Mrs. Dorman chased me out of the kitchen once with a broom," one of the twins declared.

"That was years ago," Katie said. "And she wasn't going to hit you."

"I know," the twin said. "But she still scares me."

"Do you and your mother have a housekeeper?" Katie asked.

April shook her head. "Our place isn't big enough," she replied. "We just live in the top half of a two-family house."

"Oh," a twin said. "Do you know who lives in the bottom half?"

"Sure," April said. "My aunt and uncle and cousins. My cousin Darcy's our age. She goes to the Middle School."

"Does she really?" the other twin asked. "Does she know any boys?"

"She knows lots of boys," April said. "She's very popular."

"I can't wait to meet her," the twin said. "It drives me crazy Fairfield doesn't have boys."

"We're the next street up," April said to the chauffeur. "The third house on the right."

The chauffeur parked the car right in front of April's home. April checked her block out nervously, but none of the other girls seemed to care. They ran out of the car in search of Darcy.

"I'm upstairs!" Darcy called to them. "In April's room."

So April led the girls to her bedroom. Soon they were all crammed into the room, and within moments they'd introduced themselves, much to April's relief. She hadn't known how she was going to manage Megan and Melissa's introductions.

"Tell me all about the boys at the Middle School," one of the twins said.

"What do you want to know?" Darcy asked.

"Are any of them cute?" the other twin asked.

"A few," Darcy said. "Actually the cutest one is in eighth grade. His name is Peter, and the other day he kind of brushed against me, and I think he did it on purpose. He smiled when he did it."

"Did you smile back?" Katie asked.

Darcy nodded. "Of course, I've seen him around," she said. "I see just about everybody in West Devon, when I hang out at my parents' store. They own Video To Go."

"I knew you looked familiar!" Katie cried. "I go there all the time with my mother. We rent lots of videos from you."

"Everyone in town does," Darcy said. "Video To Go has the best selection in the entire area."

"It must be exciting owning your own store," one of the twins said.

"It is, Megan," Darcy replied. April couldn't believe it. Seven seconds after she'd met them, Darcy could tell the twins apart. Megan was on the bed, which meant Melissa was sitting on the floor. As long as they never moved, April could call them by their right names. "When I was little, my parents used to take my advice about all the kiddie vids.

That's what we called them, kiddie vids. If I liked one, they bought more copies of it. Now that I'm older, they ask me all the time if I think some actor is cute or not. The ones I like, they stock up on."

"Wow," Melissa said. "We hardly get to see any videos, or even watch TV. Our father says video might kill Broadway someday, so he won't let us."

"I don't have to worry about that," Darcy said. "I'm going to be a great film director, so all my stuff'll end up on video sooner or later."

"I wish Daddy were a great film director," Megan said. "Instead of just being a stupid Broadway producer."

"Even that's better than being a surgeon," Katie said. "All my father ever does is operate on people. He cuts out gallbladders and spleens. Do you know how boring it is at supper when he tells us about another stupid spleen he cut out?"

"April's father has the best job," Melissa said. "I asked Daddy about it last night, to make sure we could be friends, and he said foreign correspondents get to live in all kinds of exotic places and meet really important people and wear trench coats. I definitely want to be a foreign correspondent when I grow up."

"Are you going to be one too?" Katie asked April. "A foreign correspondent, like your father?"

"I don't know yet," April said.

"April really should," Darcy declared. "She speaks lots of foreign languages already. And she lived in Spain for years and years."

"Did you get to see any bullfights?" Megan asked.

April shook her head. "My parents went, though," she said.

"I think I'd throw up at a bullfight," Katie said. "It'd remind me too much of all those gallbladders and spleens."

"Maybe someday I'll direct a great film about bullfights," Darcy said.

"Could I be in it?" Melissa asked.

"Melissa!" Megan shrieked.

"All right," Melissa said. "Can Megan and I be in it together? We'd love to be actresses, only Daddy says we can't. But he just means on Broadway and on TV. He never said we couldn't be movie stars."

"That's true," Megan said. "Could we be in it?"

"Sure," Darcy said. "You can play identical-twin bullfighters. When one of you gets tired, the other one runs in, and the poor bull doesn't realize it and really goes crazy."

"I don't want to be in that movie," Katie said. "Because of the gallbladders. Are you going to direct any other great movies?"

"Dozens of them," Darcy said. "I'm going to be the greatest great film director of our time."

"Wow," Katie said. "And I'll get to be in your movies. The ones without bulls."

"This is terrific," Megan said. "Tell us some more about boys, Darcy."

"Sure," Darcy said. "April, didn't your mom leave us some popcorn?"

"I'll go get it," April said. She left her bedroom, and as she walked to the kitchen, she could hear the three girls she'd invited over to be her friends become instant friends with Darcy instead.

FOUR

*I*t's easy," Darcy said as she helped herself to more rice. "Megan's left-handed and Melissa's right-handed."

April couldn't see how that would make telling the twins apart any easier, unless she constantly went up to them asking for their autographs.

"How could you tell?" Isabelle asked. The three girls and April's mother were upstairs having supper. Thursdays and Fridays, Bill and Karen both worked late at Video To Go, and Darcy and Isabelle had gotten into the habit of having supper with April and her mother. April enjoyed their company most of the time, but she was still feeling a little raw that the girls she'd picked for friends seemed to like Darcy so much more than they liked her.

"That was easy too," Darcy said. "First I noticed what a pretty watch Melissa had on. I'd love a watch like that, only it was real gold and diamonds and stuff."

"Don't hold your breath," her older sister said.

"I'll get one when I'm a great film director," Darcy replied. "Anyway, I wondered if Megan had the same watch on. They really are spooky, the way they dress exactly the same way. Robert and Rachel certainly don't."

"You mean Robert doesn't wear skirts?" April asked.

"They're not even color coordinated," Darcy declared. "Ever since you told me about Megan and Melissa, I've been checking on Robert and Rachel, and they haven't worn the same-colored shirts or anything. I guess they don't care that they're twins. So I looked for Megan's watch, and I saw it wasn't on her left hand. So I looked again, and there it was on her right hand. She does wear the identical watch, by the way, only on the wrong hand. So then I thought maybe it was a trick, or some system they had to help people tell them apart, and sometimes Megan wears her watch on her left hand and Melissa on her right just to confuse people, and I figured I'd better find out, in case April needed me to explain the system. So I asked each of them for her address and phone number, and I watched while they wrote. Megan's left-handed and Melissa's right-handed. They have the same address, but different phone numbers. I have them, April, in case you ever want to call them."

"Why would they have different phone numbers?" April's mother asked.

"I asked them," Darcy said. "They said they each had her own room, and her own number. I mean, these girls are rich."

"Rich and spoiled, it sounds like to me," Isabelle said. "Wearing gold-and-diamond watches."

"They might have just looked like gold and diamonds," April's mother said. "Darcy isn't a professional jeweler."

"I asked them about their watches too," Darcy said. "I told them Isabelle's birthday was coming soon, and maybe I could get her a watch like they had, and Megan said their watches came from Switzerland and they each cost three thousand dollars. She said their father bought them for them when his show last year got a rave review in the *New York Times*. That means it'll run forever, so he bought them watches guaranteed to run forever."

"I'd like a watch just like that," Isabelle said. "Thanks, Darcy."

"You're going to have to wait a few years," Darcy replied.

"I know," Isabelle said. "Until you're a great film director."

"Then I'll buy watches for all of us," Darcy said. "And we can all wear them on the left hand. Now you know how to tell them apart, April. Megan's left-handed and Melissa's right-handed."

April nodded, too embarrassed to admit she still had troubles with her lefts and her rights. "I'm not sure I'll be able to remember," she said.

"You need a system," Isabelle declared. "Forget about right- and left-handedness. Concentrate on the watches. Megan wears her watch on her right hand. The third letter in 'Megan' is a *g* and the third letter in 'right' is a *g*. And Melissa wears her watch on her left hand, and there's an *l* in 'left' and an *l* in 'Melissa.' "

"And 'Megan' and 'right' both have five letters," April's mother said. "You know, I can't wait to meet these girls, so I can try this system out myself."

April nodded. With her luck, the twins and Katie would prefer her mother to her too. "Did you give them your number?" she asked Darcy. "When they gave you theirs?"

Darcy shook her head. "They didn't ask for it," she said. "I guess they figured they could reach me through you, if they ever needed to. Besides, we're listed. They're not, because their father's such a big producer. He worries a lot about being bothered at home."

April felt better for a moment, until she remembered no one had asked her for her number either. Oh, well. If the twins and Katie wanted her, they could find her five days a week at Fairfield. Sitting alone, feeling sorry for herself. She'd be easy enough to spot.

The telephone rang, and April jumped right up. "I'll get it," she said, hoping that one of her new friends had indeed gone to the bother of finding her phone number. She raced over to the phone and picked it up. "Hello?" she said, trying to keep the eagerness out of her voice.

"April? Sweetie, is that you?"

"Daddy?" April cried. "Daddy? How are you?"

"I'm fine," he said. "I was hoping I'd catch you in. How are you? How's school?"

"I like it, Daddy," April said. Her father never got the long versions of things on his regular phone calls. The complicated details she always saved for letters. And a Thursday-night phone call was a rare event anyway. "How's Kenya?"

"Just fine," her father said. "I have kind of an old friend visiting me, and that's why I've called."

"Who's that, Daddy?" April asked. She didn't know most of her father's old friends because they'd lived apart for so many years.

"You ever hear of Lyon Fitzhugh?" her father asked.

"The rock star?" April said. "Of course I have. He's practically the most famous person in the world!"

April could hear her father repeat her response to his friend. "Well, he's here with me now," her father declared. "And we've been up half the night talking, and since we're both still awake, I figured I'd call you and introduce the two of you over the phone."

"Lyon Fitzhugh?" April said, not believing her luck. "How do you know him?"

"I have to admit, when I knew him, he wasn't Lyon," her father replied. "He was my friend Mark Fitzhugh's kid brother Jeffy. They lived a couple of houses down from me when we were kids. Your mother probably remembers Mark. He was at our wedding. Somewhere along the way, Jeffy dropped the Jeffy, and started using his fancy middle name. Now that I think about it, Mark had a fancy middle name too. Talbott. Yeah, we used to call him Tall Butt sometimes. That's what passed for humor when I was a kid."

"Did Lyon Fitzhugh come all the way to Kenya just to visit you?" April asked.

She could hear her father cup the phone and say something to Lyon Fitzhugh. She suspected he was repeating her question, and she could hear muffled laughter in the background. "Not exactly, sweetie," her father replied. "He's on his way to Ethiopia on a mission of mercy. There are terrible famines at settlement camps there, and he's been doing a lot of work on hunger relief, so he figured he'd fly over and check things out. But he decided to spend a couple of days in Nairobi first, and when he heard I was here, he dropped in for a visit. It's been great seeing him, catching up with old times."

"Are you going to interview him?" April asked. If her father interviewed Lyon Fitzhugh, the network would be sure to show it on the nightly news, and then she could tell everybody to watch, and people would finally believe her father was who she said he was. She bet Megan and Melissa had never met Lyon Fitzhugh. Not that she had either. Not technically, at least.

"Lyon doesn't give interviews," her father replied. "That's how he got to be so famous. By refusing to cooperate with the press. But he did say he'd like to say hello to you. Unless you have any objections, that is."

"I'd love to say hello to Lyon Fitzhugh," April declared. She could sense that her mother, Isabelle, and Darcy were all riveted by her end of the conversation. She only wished Katie and the twins had been invited for supper.

Her father handed over the phone, and sure enough, Lyon Fitzhugh got on. "Hi, April," he said. "Mitch tells me you've just started a new school. How's it going?"

April would have wet her pants except she had an audience. "It's kind of hard," she said. "Making new friends and all."

"I can imagine," Lyon Fitzhugh replied. "Sometimes it's hard for me, too, meeting new people. Like on this trip. There are a lot of people I'll have to deal with I've never met before. And I worry what they're going to think of me. Not everybody gets excited over rock musicians, you know."

"But you're not just a rock musician," April said. "You're just about the most famous rock star in the world."

Lyon Fitzhugh laughed, but it wasn't a nasty kind of laugh. "I'm big in America," he said. "But that doesn't carry much weight in Africa. Your father knows a lot more important people than I do. He's been giving me names of people I should meet, and I'm very grateful to him for that."

"Daddy knows everybody," April said. "Well, everybody in Africa, at least."

Lyon Fitzhugh laughed again. "I think he does," he said. "Well, April, it's been nice—"

But April interrupted him. "Excuse me, Mr. Fitzhugh," she said. "I know you don't give interviews, but I need to submit something to the *Fairfield Forward*—that's the school magazine—to prove to them I'm a good journalist, like my father, and could I maybe just interview you for a few minutes? I don't think they'd publish it, because they only like stuff that has a Fairfield slant, and you never went there, because it's an all-girls school, but it would give me something to show them. Please?"

"Well," Lyon Fitzhugh said. "Sure. Why not? I'd be happy to answer a couple of questions for you."

"Thank you," April said. She found the pad of

paper by the phone, where her mother always kept it, and took a deep breath. "Tell me, Mr. Fitzhugh. How long will you be in Ethiopia?"

"Are you sure you're new to this?" Lyon Fitzhugh asked. "That sounded like an awfully professional question."

"No, honest," April said. "I've never interviewed anybody before. At least not anybody famous."

"I'm going to be in Ethiopia for ten days," Lyon Fitzhugh replied. "I'd like to stay longer, but my wife and I are expecting a baby very soon, and I promised her I'd be back home in time for the delivery."

"Do you have any names picked out?" April asked.

"Derek if it's a boy," Lyon Fitzhugh replied. "Madelyn if it's a girl. April's a pretty name. I guess you were born in April."

"No, May second," April said. "But my parents were sure I'd be born in April, and they preferred it to May, so that's why I'm named April."

"Good reason," Lyon Fitzhugh said. "Any other questions?"

"What do you think you'll accomplish in Ethiopia?" April asked. She was still busy scrawling his answers to her other questions.

"Probably not very much," Lyon Fitzhugh admitted. "But I hope that my presence there will garner enough publicity to focus world attention

46

on the problem. Just because I won't give interviews to plug my latest album doesn't mean I'm publicity shy when it comes to a cause this important. If my being here, visiting the camps and talking to reporters, makes the world pay attention to the terrible tragedy going on here, then I'll gladly cooperate with the media."

"Wow," April said. "Could you hold on a second? That was kind of a long speech."

Lyon Fitzhugh laughed. "It was, wasn't it," he said. "I meant it too. Your father said he'd fly out with a crew once I settled in at the camp. So I guess you'll get to see both of us on the news next week."

"I love seeing Daddy on TV," April said. "They don't show him nearly enough."

"People forget sometimes that the third-world countries are as much a part of this planet earth as America and Europe," Lyon Fitzhugh said. "But they are. All children deserve an equal chance at health and happiness, no matter where they're born. You can quote me on that."

"Thank you," April said. "Well, I guess I should let you get back to Daddy. Have a good trip."

"Thank you," Lyon Fitzhugh said. "And good luck with your article. If for some reason that Fairfield magazine—"

"The *Forward*," April said.

"If the *Fairfield Forward* thinks there's a Fairfield slant to this interview, and they want to publish it, it's okay with me," he continued. "It might do you some good, and I don't see how it could hurt the cause any."

"Thank you," April said. "Thank you so much, Mr. Fitzhugh."

"Call me Jeff," he said. "Bye, April."

April's father picked up the phone. "Sounds like you did a great job interviewing Jeffy," he said. "Be sure to send me a copy when it gets published."

"They may not publish it," April said. "But if they do, I will."

"They'd be crazy not to," her father said. "You have a real exclusive there, the first interview with Jeffy, I mean Lyon, Fitzhugh in four or five years."

"I guess," April said. "It just might not be Fair-fieldish enough for them."

"Send me a copy anyway," her father said, "as soon as you write it. I'll show it to Jeffy, let him see how good he sounds on paper."

"All right," April said. "I love you, Daddy."

"I love you too, sweetie," he said. "I'll talk to you in a week. Take care."

"You too," she said, and hung up the phone.

"That's it!" Darcy cried. "You're in! You have your ticket to the *Forward*."

April still wasn't sure. But she knew she'd try, and that made her feel better than she had in a long time.

FIVE

Not everybody gets excited over rock stars," Lyon Fitzhugh, maybe the most famous rock star in the world, admitted yesterday, from Nairobi, Kenya, where he was visiting his boyhood friend, Mitchell Hughes, father of seventh-grader April Hughes.

Mr. Fitzhugh, who old friends call Jeffy, is on his way to Ethiopia to visit camps and check on their conditions. He is hoping that his visit there will focus world attention on the problem of famine. Although Mr. Fitzhugh doesn't like to give interviews, he says he isn't publicity shy when it comes to important causes. "If my being here, visiting the camps and talking to reporters, makes the world pay attention to the terrible tragedy going on here, then I'll gladly cooperate with the media."

Mr. Fitzhugh has been concerned about life in third-world countries for a long time. "People forget

49

sometimes that third-world countries are as much a part of this planet earth as America and Europe," he said in this exclusive interview. "But they are. All children deserve an equal chance at health and happiness, no matter where they're born."

Mr. Fitzhugh is going to be in Ethiopia for ten days, and then will be flying home to be with his wife when she has their baby. They're going to name it Derek if it's a boy, and Madelyn if it's a girl. While he's in Ethiopia, he'll probably be on the DBC nightly news a lot, with Mitchell Hughes.

April stood still as both Brooke and Mrs. Holcomb read her article. She knew it wasn't perfect, didn't sound exactly the way a real newspaper article would, and probably didn't have enough of a Fairfield slant for the *Forward* to publish it. But she hoped it was good enough for them to give her a shot at another assignment.

She realized she was more nervous with them than she had been actually talking to Lyon Fitzhugh. But then again, her father wasn't around to call either of them Jeffy. April pictured Brooke being called Jeffy and tried not to giggle.

"Lyon Fitzhugh really talked to you?" Brooke asked when she finished reading the piece.

It hadn't occurred to April that anyone would doubt that. "Of course he did," she said, her cheeks turning red from the unspoken accusation. "I don't lie. He was visiting my father."

"I thought he never gave interviews," Brooke continued. "Why was he with your father if he doesn't give interviews?"

"Daddy wasn't interviewing him," April replied. "I was. He knows Daddy because they lived on the same block when they were kids. And he said I could interview him for the *Fairfield Forward*. He said he wouldn't even mind if you published it, if it had enough of a Fairfield slant."

"He is in Africa," Mrs. Holcomb said. "I read that in the papers a couple of days ago. And the article mentioned that his wife was expecting a baby soon."

"You can call Nairobi and ask my father," April said. "Except he'll probably call him Jeffy."

Mrs. Holcomb smiled. "I don't think that's necessary," she declared. "I think we have an authentic interview here with a man who almost never grants any. Congratulations, April. What do you intend to do with it?"

"You mean the *Forward* won't publish it?" April asked.

"We'd be delighted to," Mrs. Holcomb said. "I think it has enough of a Fairfield slant to it. But you might be able to sell it someplace else."

April thought quickly about how famous she could become if she sold her exclusive Lyon Fitzhugh interview to some big magazine or newspaper. Everyone in school would want to know her then. The whole town would hear about her. Even

Megan and Melissa's producer father would be impressed.

But Lyon Fitzhugh hadn't agreed to that. "It's for the *Forward*," she said with a sigh. "That's what he agreed to."

"We'll be sure to publish it in our first issue," Mrs. Holcomb said. "If that's all right with you, Brooke."

"It needs a little work," Brooke said. "You still have a lot to learn about journalism, April."

"I know," April said, but not even Brooke's know-it-all attitude could bother her just then. "But I'm willing to learn. Do you think you could give me another assignment and I could learn from that?"

"I think she's earned that," Mrs. Holcomb said to Brooke. "What do you have available?"

"The alumna piece," Brooke said. "Every issue we try to interview an alumna. Do you know what an alumna is?"

For a moment April thought it was someone who worked with tin foil, but then she remembered. "Someone who graduated," she said.

For the first time, Brooke seemed impressed. "Most new girls don't know that," she said. "We try to find an alumna in the area who's doing something interesting with her life, so she can be kind of an inspiration to us. A lot of girls here just plan to lead the kinds of lives their mothers lead. You know, country clubs, golf games, nothing interesting. So we try to find alumnae who are doing something more than that, and maybe we can get a girl or two to change her mind and become a lawyer or something."

"My mother's a nurse practitioner," April said. "But I don't want to be one of those."

"That's still better than playing golf all day long," Brooke declared.

"Who's our alumna for this month?" Mrs. Holcomb asked.

Brooke looked at her list. "How about Jennifer March?" she said. "April might do really well with her because of the TV connection."

"Is she a TV star?" April asked. She'd never heard of Jennifer March, but ever since she and her mother had moved in with Darcy's family, they never watched plain TV except for the news. Instead they watched videos from Video To Go. Sometimes April flat-out missed commercials.

"She's a reporter," Brooke said, "with the West Devon cable TV station. Channel Six. She graduated from Fairfield seven years ago, and then she went to Northwestern University for her bachelor's, and Syracuse for her master's, and now she's back here. I've seen her a couple of times. She's okay."

"She was a very bright student," Mrs. Holcomb said. "A former editor of the *Forward*, as a matter of fact. And she's agreed to be interviewed. Why don't I give you her number, and you can set up an appointment."

"That would be great," April said. Her first real interview. Talking to Lyon Fitzhugh on the phone probably didn't count. Face-to-face was the real test.

Mrs. Holcomb looked up the number, then wrote it down for April. "It looks like you'll have two pieces in this issue of the *Forward*," she said. "That has to be a record for a seventh-grader."

"Just don't ask Jennifer March any dumb questions," Brooke said. "Remember, you're representing Fairfield."

April wanted to say how impressed Lyon Fitzhugh had been with her questions, but she was afraid it would sound like bragging. "I'll try not to," she said instead. "I'll call her as soon as I get home. Thank you."

"Thank you, April," Mrs. Holcomb said.

April ran home, her book bag swinging merrily. She was on the staff of the *Forward*. Wait until Katie and Melissa and Megan heard. They'd all be so impressed, they'd become friends with her right away.

But her good mood vanished the moment she entered the house. She could hear voices from Darcy's apartment. Darcy must have heard her as well, because she opened the door, grabbed April, and said, "Come on in."

So April did. As always, she was shocked by how

messy Darcy's home was. There were books, magazines, and videos tossed everywhere. There was a plate with a half a dozen chocolate-chip cookies on it resting on the floor, and not for the first time April envied Darcy her parents' acceptance of junk food. The only treat waiting for April was apples.

"Hi, April."

April turned around and saw Megan and Melissa sitting in the living room. They were poring over a pile of videos and hardly looked up at her.

"Hi," she said.

"Where were you?" Darcy asked. "Megan and Melissa came over right after school."

"Were they waiting for me?" April whispered.

"Sure, sort of," Darcy said.

"We wanted to see all of Darcy's videos," Megan (or was it Melissa?) said. April wished they'd at least flash their watches, so she could tell one from the other. "The ones she's made."

"You mean those stupid ones we did during the summer?" April asked. The ones she had starred in. If the twins saw them, she would die.

"They weren't stupid," Darcy said. "Low budget maybe, but not stupid."

"We watched one of them," Melissa or maybe Megan said. "You played a mother and a doll was your baby and you were giving it up for adoption."

"That was nothing," April said. "I mean, Darcy just told me what to do and I did it. I don't play with dolls anymore."

"We could tell it was acting," the twin said. April forced herself to stare at her wrist. Watch on the left. That meant she was either Megan or Melissa. Melissa. Left was Melissa. Not that April was going to risk it by calling her anything.

"I liked the way Darcy held the camera," Megan, watch on right, said. "It hardly wobbled or anything."

"Naturally when I'm a great film director someone else will hold the camera," Darcy said. "Sometimes Isabelle does it for me, but mostly she likes to recite her poetry while I do the taping. I have lots of tape of her if you want to be bored."

The twins giggled. April no longer cared which one was which.

"I have good news," she said. "I got an assignment for the *Forward*. From the *Forward*, I mean. I don't know. But I'm going to interview someone. An alumna. You know what that is?"

The twins laughed. "They gave you that job?" Megan asked.

"That's the worst job on the *Forward*," Melissa said.

"No one reads the alumna interviews," Megan said.

"They're boring," Melissa said.

"Oh," April said.

"It won't be boring when April's through with it," Darcy declared. "She's a really good writer. She's interviewed all kinds of famous people."

"No I haven't," April said.

"You interviewed Lyon Fitzhugh," Darcy said. "Yesterday. On the telephone."

"*The* Lyon Fitzhugh?" Megan said.

"The rock star?" Melissa said.

"That's the one," Darcy said.

"How did you meet him?" Megan asked.

"I didn't exactly meet him," April replied. "He was in Nairobi, visiting my father, and they called, and I interviewed him on the phone."

"Daddy doesn't even know Lyon Fitzhugh," Melissa said. "But he'd like to. He says if Lyon Fitzhugh would just star in a Broadway show, it could save Broadway from video. No insult intended, Darcy."

"That's okay," Darcy said. "April interviewed him on the telephone and wrote a wonderful article all about it. Do you have a copy on you, April, to show them?"

April shook her head. "I left my copy at school," she said. "They said it had enough of a Fairfield slant so they'd publish it."

"That's great!" Darcy said. "And now you're going to interview someone else, too—whatever it was you said."

"An alumna," April said. "I guess that's the kind of assignment they give to seventh-graders." She could believe that Brooke would saddle her with a dumb assignment, but not Mrs. Holcomb. Maybe Mrs. Holcomb didn't know that nobody read the alumna interviews.

"Who are you going to interview?" Darcy asked. "Somebody real exciting, I bet."

"Jennifer March," April said. "She's on the Channel Six news."

Darcy nodded. "Because your father's on the news too," she said. "Good choice. They must really know what they're doing on the *Fairfield Forward*."

But the twins no longer seemed interested. "We should be going," Melissa declared. "The car should be coming around any moment now."

"They could only stay for an hour," Darcy said. "I was sure you'd be home sooner than that."

"I had to wait a while for Brooke and Mrs. Holcomb to see me," April said.

"There's the car," Megan said, peeking out of the window. "Bye, Darcy. Thanks for letting us see your videos."

"Bye, Darcy," Melissa said. The twins grabbed their books and left.

They didn't even say good-bye to me, April thought. She didn't know what was worst, the way they'd visited Darcy and not her, or the way they insulted the job she'd been assigned by the *Forward,* or the way they hadn't even bothered to say good-bye.

"They're kind of weird," Darcy said. "I didn't invite them over, April."

"I didn't think you had," April said.

"I just got home from school, and then there they

were," Darcy said. "Driving up here in that silly limo of theirs. I don't know what the neighbors are going to think. I mean, once I'm a great film director, they'll have to get used to seeing limos in the neighborhood all the time, but not yet."

April nodded.

"And then they said they wanted to see my videos, so of course I showed some of them," Darcy said. "I hope you don't mind."

"It's okay," April said. "Look, Darcy, I'd better go upstairs. I have to call Jennifer March and make an appointment with her."

"I think it's terrific that they gave you an assignment," Darcy said. "And even if nobody does read those whatdoyoucallems—"

"Alumna interviews," April said.

"Yeah, those," Darcy said. "You'll do such a good job, everybody'll read them. I bet the *New York Times*'ll hire you before you're in eighth grade."

"Darcy," April said.

"Or better yet, you'll end up on TV," Darcy said, "interviewing people there. You can grill them and make them confess to all kinds of crimes. And everybody in America'll know you. You'll be as famous as me. I'll be a great film director and you'll be a great TV interviewer. We'll end up on the covers of every magazine in America."

"I'm going upstairs now," April said.

Darcy didn't even hear. "I'll make a movie about

you," she said. "A documentary. *A Day in the Life of April Hughes, Great TV Interviewer*. I'll win an Oscar for that too, for best documentary—"

April let out a deep breath and walked up the stairs to her home. Darcy could continue to fantasize as much as she wanted. April knew the truth. She was doomed to a life of boring nothingness. She might as well start with the golf lessons right away, since that was all she'd do until she was an old, old lady.

*T*hank you for seeing me, Ms. March," April said Saturday morning.

Jennifer March stared at her. "You look awfully young," she declared. "Shouldn't you be home watching cartoon shows?"

April shook her head. "They assigned me to you. Or you to me." She blushed. "I mean, Mrs. Holcomb, she's the teacher-advisor. . . ."

"She was the teacher-advisor when I worked on the *Forward*," Jennifer March said. "She's been the teacher-advisor since before the Flood."

April wasn't sure which flood Jennifer March meant, but since she'd lived in West Devon a lot longer than April had, it must have been one a long time before. She immediately thought "Wet Devon," and bit down a nervous giggle.

"I'm sorry," Jennifer March said. "Sit down. I

guess I was expecting an older girl to interview me, that's all. I used to work on the *Forward,* you know. I was editor my senior year, and it felt like a big deal to me when they asked if I'd be willing to be an alumna profile. I don't get a lot of respect here, at Channel Six. I'm new, and my uncle owns the station, so they don't know how good I am yet. But I'm good, and this is just a stepping stone in my career. I expect to end up on one of the networks someday, maybe even anchoring the nightly news." She smiled at the thought.

April tried to write down everything Jennifer March had just said, but she knew she hadn't gotten it all. There had to be an easier way to interview people, she decided, and if she continued to do it, she'd figure it out. "Did you like Fairfield?" she asked, just in case they needed the slant.

"It was a good school," Jennifer March replied. "Naturally I missed boys. How do you like it?"

"I don't know yet," April said. "I just started a few days ago."

"Oh," Jennifer March said. "You mean they sent a new girl to interview me?"

"I guess they had their reasons," April replied. "Maybe because my father's on TV."

"What does he do?" Jennifer March asked.

"He's the Africa correspondent for DBC," April said. "He lives in Nairobi. That's in Kenya."

"I know where Nairobi is," Jennifer March declared. She looked like she did too. "I guess he doesn't come to West Devon a lot."

"He's never been here," April said. "No, that isn't true. He must have come when I was little, and my parents were still married, because that's where my aunt and uncle live, so he probably came to visit them, only I don't remember. We lived in Madrid for a while, and then they got divorced, and I don't remember much of what was before Spain."

"If your parents are divorced, I guess your father'll never come to West Devon," Jennifer March said.

April shrugged. "He gets some vacation time," she replied. "He got the first two weeks of July off this summer, and I went to London and met him there."

"You must lead a pretty glamorous life," Jennifer March said. "Do you ever get to meet any network-news executives?"

April was aware that Jennifer March was doing the interviewing. It hadn't been that way with Lyon Fitzhugh. "I guess I've met some," she said. "Only the ones at DBC, though."

Jennifer March smiled at her. "West Devon must seem like quite a letdown for you," she said. "London. Madrid. Do you want to do television news when you grow up?"

"I don't know yet," April said. "So do you like your job? Here, I mean. What exactly do you do?"

"I do some investigative work," Jennifer March replied. "But it's hard, since my family is so connected, if you know what I mean. My father's a bank president, my uncle's a judge. It just wouldn't be right for me to investigate them, or any of the businesses they're connected with. Not that any of them would do anything wrong. But still, I'm kind of stuck. I really don't know how long I'll stay here, especially since they mostly give me fluff pieces. Old ladies turning one hundred. Couples married seventy years. Spelling bees. Science fairs. That's not what I got my masters for."

"So your job is pretty boring," April said as she scribbled.

"Not boring," Jennifer March replied. "I still have a lot to learn, and I can learn while I cover spelling bees. It's just not as challenging as I'd hoped for. But your father must have told you stories about his early years in journalism, how he worked his way up."

"All he says is he always wanted to report on Africa, and there weren't that many people who always wanted to report on Africa, so when there was an opening, they gave it to him," April said. "That's why he and my mom got divorced, because she didn't want to live in Africa and he wanted to. First they fought, and then they got a divorce. Are your parents divorced?"

Jennifer March shook her head. "Still married," she said.

"And do you have any brothers or sisters?"

"One brother," she replied. "He got his M.B.A. at Harvard, and he's working with Daddy at the bank."

"Sounds nice," April said.

"Basically my family's boring," Jennifer March declared. "Nice enough, but boring. It's no trick to own a town the size of West Devon. It's owning New York or L.A. that's the trick."

"Do you think it matters where you come from?" April asked. "Do you have to come from New York to own New York?"

"Probably not," Jennifer March replied. "But I'd rather my uncle owned DBC than Channel Six. I'd get ahead a lot faster that way."

"I don't know," April said. "My father's just from Wisconsin, and he's on the news whenever something important happens in Africa. I bet he'll even be on tonight, because Lyon Fitzhugh is there. That's what Lyon Fitzhugh told me anyway, that Daddy would be on the news a lot covering his trip."

"You know Lyon Fitzhugh?" Jennifer March asked.

"I interviewed him," April said. "A couple of days ago."

"Nobody interviews Lyon Fitzhugh," Jennifer March said. "He doesn't give interviews."

"He kind of did it as a favor," April said. "I needed something with a Fairfield slant to convince them I could write for the *Forward*. And Daddy called from Nairobi, and he and Lyon Fitzhugh were spending the evening together, because they lived on the same block in Wisconsin when they were growing up, and I asked Lyon Fitzhugh if I could interview him and he said okay. He was really nice. He answered all my questions and said I could quote him and everything."

"Lyon Fitzhugh," Jennifer March said. "I went to one of his concerts when I was at Syracuse, and he was amazing. I guess you'll never get to meet him."

"I don't think so," April said. "But you see, he's from Wisconsin, and he's famous. So I think even if you come from West Devon, you could maybe end up anchoring the nightly news in New York if you're good enough."

"You have to make your own breaks," Jennifer March declared. "Nobody does it for you. You can't just sit around and wait for them to happen."

"Oh," April said. She didn't think it would be polite to ask if having an uncle who owned the business was the kind of break you made for yourself. "So what was your favorite subject at school? Fairfield, I mean."

"English," Jennifer March said. "At least that's what I did best in. I liked history a lot too."

April nodded. At last she'd gotten an answer that was easy to write down. "And what did you like best about Fairfield?"

"I don't know," Jennifer March replied. "I went there from kindergarten through high school. It was just like home. After a while, you take it for granted."

April had lived in too many places to take home for granted. She still remembered how strange it felt to move to a place where people spoke English, not Spanish. "Do you keep in touch with your friends?" she asked. "Your friends from Fairfield, I mean."

"You know, when I did those stupid alumna interviews, I never asked questions like that," Jennifer March declared. "I can't tell whether you're very good or just very naive."

"I'm interested," April said. "That's all."

"What kind of questions did you ask Lyon Fitzhugh?" Jennifer March asked.

"Stuff about Africa," April said. "And what they were going to name their baby. Derek if it's a boy and Madelyn if it's a girl. I mean, that was his answer. I didn't ask him if he was going to name it Derek or Madelyn. What do you think you'll name your kids, if you have any."

"I'm not sure I'll have any," Jennifer March said. "Motherhood is such a trap. It ties you down. What if your mother had been the one who wanted to go to Africa? Do you think she could have if you were around?"

"I don't know," April said. She decided she didn't want to talk to Jennifer March about her mother. "Do you have any words of advice for Fairfield students?" she asked. The question sounded dumb to her, but her uncle Bill insisted she ask. He said people loved to give advice, especially people in their twenties.

"Just to work hard and apply themselves," Jennifer March said. "And to do whatever it takes to make it to the top. Not to settle, if you know what I mean. Never get too complacent. Do you know what complacent means?"

"Satisfied," April said. "Smug."

"That's it exactly," Jennifer March said. "A school like Fairfield, a town like West Devon, they manufacture complacent people. But I want something more out of life, and I think all the girls who go to Fairfield should want that something more as well."

April had the uncomfortable feeling that Jennifer March would continue to give advice for hours unless she did something to stop her. So she did. She rose from her chair and said, "Thank you."

"Thank you," Jennifer March replied. "No, I mean that. You made me look at myself, at my goals, and I'm grateful. That doesn't happen often, that you have that chance to really evaluate who you are, where you're going. I think you're going to be an excellent reporter someday, April. My guess is you take after your father."

"I hope so," April said, although now that she'd actually interviewed someone, she was thinking

68

more and more about becoming a doctor. "Thanks again."

"Keep in touch," Jennifer March said. "And if your father should ever visit you here, please let me know. I'd love to meet him."

"Sure," April said. She put her notepad in her pocket and left the TV station. It wasn't much of a TV station, not compared to the DBC network station in New York her father had taken her to a few times. But West Devon wasn't New York, as Jennifer March kept saying.

She walked back home trying to decide what kind of doctor to be. Katie's father was a surgeon, but that only seemed to be about gallbladders, and April didn't think she wanted to spend the rest of her life with those, whatever they did. Maybe she should cure illnesses instead, like blindness or cancer. If she cured stuff like that, then she'd be even more famous than Darcy the great film director. She wondered if scientists ever got awards like Oscars. Maybe she'd just be Miss America instead. They were famous for a while.

Darcy heard her when she got home, and opened the door to her apartment. "Come on in," she said. "Everybody's here."

April peeked in, afraid she'd find the twins and Katie. But instead there were Darcy's own friends, girls who went to the Middle School with her. "I don't think so," she said. "I think I want to write up my interview while it's still fresh in my mind."

"How'd it go?" Darcy asked. She turned to her friends and said, "April just interviewed Jennifer March. She's on the Channel Six news."

"She's a real no-talent," one of the girls said. "That's what my father says. He says if her father didn't own the TV station, she'd never get a job."

"Her uncle," April said. "Not her father."

"Uncle, father, same thing," the girl said. "That's how it is in West Devon. It's not who you are. It's who you know."

"I know everybody in West Devon," Darcy declared. "That's because they all take out videos in Video To Go. Sure you don't want to come in?"

"Positive," April said. She never felt comfortable with Darcy's friends. It would have been different if they went to the same school, but since they didn't, the only thing they had in common was Darcy, and that wasn't enough. "I'll see you later," she said. "Bye."

She walked up the stairs and opened the door to her apartment.

"Hi, honey," April's mother said from the kitchen. "How did the interview go?"

"Okay, I guess," April replied, joining her. "She seemed interested in me, because of Daddy I think."

"That makes sense," April's mother replied. "Your father's a network-news correspondent, and Jennifer March does local news for a local station. Naturally she'd be impressed."

"She said there's a lot you can learn from cov-

70

ering spelling bees, but I don't think she meant it," April said, taking an apple from the refrigerator.

"Wash it first," her mother said.

"I know," April said. She gave it a quick shower, then bit into it. "Mom, when you were a kid, did you have trouble making friends?"

"Not that I can remember," her mother said. She looked up from the newspaper she'd been reading. "Why? Are you having trouble?"

April scowled. "I just wish I could make friends faster," she said. "The way Darcy does."

"Darcy's more outgoing than you," April's mother replied. "You'll be sure to make friends soon. You're doing the right thing, working on the *Forward*. You'll get to know other girls interested in journalism, and pretty soon you'll have plenty of friends."

April wondered if she should break it to her mother that she was no longer interested in journalism and had decided to become a doctor instead. Her mother didn't always like doctors, at least not the ones who didn't like nurse practitioners. She decided it could wait.

"I should probably write up this interview," she said. "Jennifer March said some interesting stuff about not getting too complacent. That was her advice. Uncle Bill was right. She loved giving advice."

April's mother smiled. "Go to it then," she said. "Let me see it when you're done."

"Okay," April said. She finished the apple, tossed the core in the garbage, and was about to go to her room when the phone rang. She picked it up.

"April? This is Jennifer March."

"Yeah?" April said.

"It just came over the wires," Jennifer March declared. "Lyon Fitzhugh's plane is missing. Could you come down to the station right away? You were one of the last people in America to talk to him, and I want to interview you for my news show."

SEVEN

*A*t six o'clock Karen, Isabelle, and Darcy gathered in April's apartment along with April and her mother to watch the Channel Six news. Only Bill was missing, and he said he'd be sure to watch on one of the sets at Video To Go. The VCR was set in both apartments to tape the news. April would keep one copy, and the other would be sent to her father. April was a nervous wreck.

"I really sounded dumb," she warned everybody in the room.

"You never sound dumb," Isabelle replied. "Unlike Darcy."

"I take after my big sister that way," Darcy said.

Karen and Joanne laughed. "They sound just like we did," Joanne declared. "I'm so glad I have an only child."

April laughed along with the others, but it was

a nervous laugh. She'd never been on TV before, at least not being interviewed for a news show about a major international news event. She knew nobody watched Channel Six, but it still felt important to her. She just wished it was over with already. No matter how bad she was, she knew her family would say she was great, and she was willing to accept the lies.

"In international news today, an airplane carrying rock star Lyon Fitzhugh and several relief workers is missing in Ethiopia," the Channel Six news anchor announced. "A faint radio signal has been detected, but it may take days before the site of the accident is located. Until then the world waits to find out if there are any survivors from the flight. Eight people were believed to be on board. We will have more information as this continuing story develops.

"Locally, a twelve-year-old girl living in West Devon is believed to be among the last Americans to speak to Fitzhugh. April Hughes, a student at Fairfield Academy, had a telephone conversation with Fitzhugh on Thursday. Jennifer March is here with the story."

They cut to Jennifer, who looked older somehow than she had when April had interviewed her. April knew roughly what was coming next, and began to blush.

"April Hughes, a seventh-grader at Fairfield Academy, is the daughter of Mitchell Hughes, Africa correspondent for DBC News," Jennifer began. "She's used to meeting celebrities. But even April was excited when the phone rang on Thursday evening and the voice on the other side was that of internationally beloved rock-star Lyon Fitzhugh."

And there was a shot of April, fidgeting in a chair. At least she was dressed nicely, she thought, since she'd still had on the outfit she'd worn to interview Jennifer March that morning.

"You look beautiful," Darcy said.

"Shush," Isabelle said.

"April, what was your exact reaction when you heard Lyon Fitzhugh's voice over the phone?" Jennifer March asked on the TV set.

"I guess I said hello," April replied. The real April shut her eyes and wished she were in Ethiopia.

Jennifer March smiled. April peeked, and noticed Jennifer March hadn't smiled that way when April had been doing the interviewing. "Were you excited?" she asked.

"Oh, yeah," the TV April said. "I'd never met Lyon Fitzhugh."

"And why was Lyon calling you?" Jennifer March asked.

"He was an old friend of my father's," April said. "They grew up on the same block together. My father called him Jeffy, because Lyon's just his middle name."

"What did you and Lyon talk about?" Jennifer March asked. At least she didn't call him Jeffy.

"We talked about my new school," April said. "Fairfield, and whether I liked it, and I told him I wanted to write for the magazine there, the *Fairfield Forward,* and could I interview him, since they probably wouldn't print it because it wouldn't have a Fairfield slant. He doesn't give interviews, you know."

"I know," Jennifer March said, as though she'd tried several times to get Lyon Fitzhugh to agree to one. "What did he say to your request?"

"He was real nice," April said. "He said they could even publish it if it had enough of a Fairfield slant for them. And Mrs. Holcomb, she's the teacher-advisor—oh that's right, you know that—anyway, she said it did after she read it, so it's going to be in the *Fairfield Forward.*"

"I'm going to die," April moaned from the living-room sofa.

"Shush," her entire family said.

"So you interviewed Lyon Fitzhugh," Jennifer March said. "What kinds of questions did you ask?"

"How long he was going to be in Ethiopia," April said. "And he said ten days, because he'd promised his wife he'd be back before she had their baby. They're going to name it Derek if it's a boy, and Madelyn if it's a girl. I guess I asked him that too. And then I asked him what he was hoping to accomplish in Ethiopia, because that's the kind of question my father asks."

"And Lyon's response to that was?" Jennifer March said.

"He said he didn't really think he'd accomplish very much, but it was important to focus world attention on the problem of famine," April said. The real April looked up. She didn't sound nearly so stupid anymore. "He said just because he didn't give interviews about his own work didn't mean he'd avoid publicity about something that was important. He said if it took his going to the camps and talking to reporters for the world to notice, then he'd do it. And I knew he was right, because he said my father would be flying out later with a crew to take shots just like that." April was silent for a moment, and Jennifer March let her be. "I'm glad my father wasn't on that flight," she said. "He called us this afternoon to tell us he was flying to Ethiopia to work on the story, and as soon as he heard anything about Lyon Fitzhugh, he'd be sure to let us know."

"So you may well be the first person in America contacted about the fate of Lyon Fitzhugh," Jennifer March declared.

"I don't think so," April said. "There're going to be lots of reporters there trying to find him too. And Daddy'll probably call the network before he calls me."

April's mother smiled at her. "You are a very smart girl," she said.

April blushed again, but this time not from embarrassment.

"Did Lyon Fitzhugh have any final words for you," Jennifer March asked, "when you spoke to him just two nights ago?"

April on TV nodded. "He said people forget that third-world countries are as much a part of this planet as America is," she said. "He said children there deserve the same chance at health and happiness. And then he said I could quote him on that."

"And you just did, most eloquently," Jennifer March said. "Thank you, April. I'm sure your prayers are with Lyon Fitzhugh this moment, as are the prayers of many millions of people who have never had the opportunity of meeting that great rock star and man."

"In other news today," the Channel Six anchor said, and Karen turned the sound down on the TV.

"You were wonderful," April's mother said.

"You really were," Aunt Karen said. "So self-assured."

The telephone rang. April ran to pick it up.

"I just saw you on TV," her uncle Bill said. "So did everybody else at the shop. And we all thought you were great. You have a real future on TV news, if you're interested."

April still hadn't given up on the idea of curing

blindness, but she thanked him anyway. As soon as she hung up the phone, it rang again.

"Hi, April."

"Hi, April."

"Who is this?" she asked.

"Megan and Melissa," the twins said. Since April couldn't see their watches, there was absolutely no way of telling them apart.

"We saw you on the news," they said. "We watched with Daddy. He was very impressed too. He said he hopes we invite you over for supper sometime when he's home, which he almost never is for supper because of his being a Broadway producer."

"Yes," April said. She didn't know what else to say.

"You looked very pretty," one twin declared.

"And you sounded smart," the other twin said.

"So do you think you could come over for dinner sometime?" the twins asked.

"Sometime, sure," April said.

"Good," the twins said. "We'll check Daddy's appointment book and set up a date."

April hung up the phone, only to hear it ring again. She didn't know how many more shocks her nervous system could take.

"April, this is Mrs. Holcomb. I just wanted to say I saw you on the news, and I thought you were wonderful."

"Thank you, Mrs. Holcomb," April said. She wished there was a chair right by the phone, since she was feeling an ever greater need to sit down.

"I especially enjoyed your comments about the *Fairfield Forward*," Mrs. Holcomb said. "And I loved it when you mentioned my name."

"I just answered her questions," April said. "I guess she knew what to ask because she'd gone to Fairfield too."

Mrs. Holcomb laughed. "Whatever the reason, I was very proud of you both," she said. "And I can't wait to see your interview with Jennifer."

"I'll write it tomorrow," April said. She hung up the phone, and this time it took almost thirty seconds before it rang again.

"Your line's been busy," the voice said. "This is Katie."

"Hi, Katie," April said. "What's up?"

"I just saw you on TV," Katie said. "I watched with my mom and dad. They both said you seemed very smart. Dad said you obviously had compassion, and maybe you should think about becoming a doctor."

"Maybe I will," April said.

"I was wondering if you'd like to have lunch with me on Monday," Katie said. "Unless you already have people you eat lunch with."

"Lunch Monday sounds okay," April said. She hung up the phone and then took the receiver off, so if anybody else tried calling, all they'd get was a busy signal. "Did you hear that?" she asked her family. "I just got phone calls from everybody."

"Of course you did," her mother said. "That's how good you were."

"But how did they know to watch?" April asked. "Nobody watches Channel Six."

"I kind of made some phone calls," Darcy said.

"You kind of did *what?*" April said.

"First I called the twins," Darcy replied. "I had their phone numbers, remember, to see if they were really right- and left-handed. And I told them you were going to be on, and then they gave me Katie's number, so I called her, and then I looked up all the Holcombs in the phone book, and there were only three, so I called until I got the right one, which was number two, by the way. I bet the number-one Holcomb watched you on the news too, because I talked to her for a few minutes about why I was trying to find the right Mrs. Holcomb, and it turned out she was the right Mrs. Holcomb's sister-in-law. That's why the right Mrs. Holcomb was number two, because her sister-in-law gave me the number. Otherwise she would have been number three, because she was third in the phone book. So it was a good thing I got the wrong Mrs. Holcomb first. Of course, if I'd gotten the wrong Mrs. Holcomb second, then maybe the first wrong Mrs. Holcomb would have watched you on TV too. Oh, well."

"I don't believe you," April said. "Why did you do all that, make those phone calls?"

"Because I thought you'd want everyone to see you on TV," Darcy replied. "I'd want everyone to see me, if I was on TV, so I told everybody. Why? Didn't you want everyone to know?"

April wasn't sure. On the one hand, she was still embarrassed, convinced that in the beginning of the interview at least, she'd sounded really stupid. On the other hand, it was nice that all those people saw her on TV, and were impressed with her, and wanted to have lunch with her, and supper, and introduce her to their Broadway-producer father.

"I would have called that Brooke person, but I didn't know her last name," Darcy said. "So I called all my friends instead, to tell them, but I guess they weren't as interested. If you'd hang out with them more, they'd have watched too, I bet."

"That's okay," April said. "I don't need the whole world to see me."

"Hear that, Darcy?" Isabelle asked. "Not everybody needs the world to stop in its tracks and admire her."

"I don't need it either," Darcy said. "I can be a great film director and nobody'll know and that'll still be okay. At least until I win my first Oscar. Then they'd better notice me."

"They'll notice you long before then," April's mother said. "If you don't become a great film director, maybe you should think about becoming a great press agent. You seem to have a gift for publicity."

"I don't think so," Darcy said. "I was just doing it as a favor for April. It was a favor, April. I hope you're not mad or anything."

"I'm not mad," April said. "Did you all really think I was okay?"

"You were a lot better than that," Aunt Karen said. "You were calm and mature, and frankly, you seemed a whole lot smarter than Jennifer March."

"I thought she was okay," Isabelle said. "Jennifer March, I mean. I thought April was wonderful, but Jennifer March seemed to know what questions to ask."

"Well, we rehearsed kind of first," April said. "She asked me about my conversation with Lyon, and she took notes, and then when the cameras were running, she already knew what my answers were going to be. I think that made it easier for her."

"She did a very professional job," April's mother said. "And so did you, April. Your father is going to be thrilled when he has a chance to see the videotape."

"I guess that won't be for a while," April said. "Not until they find the airplane." The whole room fell silent as they thought about the event that had catapulted April to fame. "Do you think he's okay?" April asked. "Lyon, I mean, and the other people on his plane?"

"I hope so," her mother said. "And no news is good news."

"His poor wife," Isabelle said. "I hope she isn't alone."

"I hope the media don't eat her up," Aunt Karen said. "They can be such vultures at times. Not Mitch, of course, but the others."

"Mitch too," April's mother said. "It goes with the job."

April walked back to the telephone and hung it up again, so if her father called, she'd be able to answer. When it rang almost immediately, she jumped.

"Hello, April. This is Jennifer March. Were you pleased with the interview?"

"Yes, I was," April said. "We were just talking about it, how good you were and everything."

"Thank you," Jennifer March said. "I wanted to tell you. Channel Six has sold the interview to the Continual News Network. They're going to run it at different points all tonight, and tomorrow as well. Do you have cable?"

"Yes, we do," April said.

"Then you'll be able to see yourself at the same time as millions of people all over the world," Jennifer March declared. "Congratulations, April. This is a big move for both of us."

EIGHT

"April!"

"Oh, April!"

"I saw you on the news yesterday, April."

"April, is it true you really know Lyon Fitz-hugh?"

"April, what have you heard about Lyon Fitz-hugh?"

"April, you were on the news yesterday."

"April, did you know? You were on the news all day yesterday."

"Want to have lunch, April?"

"Are you busy after school, April?"

"Want to be my partner for the science project, April?"

"Come sit next to me, April."

April sighed. The whole day had been like that. Of course, the day before, she'd gotten over a dozen phone calls, some of them from Fairfield girls she was just barely aware of herself, girls she knew had never known she existed. But at least half the calls had come from people she knew all over the country who'd seen her on the Continual News Network. They were just excited to see an old friend, and it was fun talking with them, catching up on things.

The other phone calls, the ones from Fairfield girls, felt weird, though, and having everybody at school fawn over her felt even weirder. Before she'd become a celebrity, nobody cared. But now that she'd been on TV, talking about her conversation with Lyon Fitzhugh, she couldn't keep them away.

"Come on, April, sit next to me," Katie said at lunchtime. April followed her to the table Katie always ate at, surrounded by the twins and her other friends.

"April should sit between us," Melissa said. "We want to talk to her about Daddy."

"April's supposed to have supper with us," Megan declared. "So it's important she sit between us."

"But she said she'd have lunch with me," Katie said. "Didn't you, April?"

"I did," April said. "Sorry."

"Then sit across from us," Megan said. "And we can talk to you across the table."

"I want to talk to her too," Annabelle Williams said. She was in half of April's classes and had never before that day even grunted in April's direction. "I want to hear all about Lyon Fitzhugh."

"We all want to hear about Lyon Fitzhugh," Maggie Loomis declared. She was in the other half of April's classes and had actually grunted once in April's direction. "Get out of my way," she'd muttered once, or maybe it was "Do you mind?"

"I don't know anything about him," April said.

"Have you heard from your father?" Megan asked.

"We saw him on the news last night," Melissa said. "Daddy watched with us. He said he had a real presence."

"He said your father should be on Broadway," Megan said. "That it would be a real casting coup to get a genuine TV reporter to act in a play. He said your father should definitely give him a call the next time he was home from Africa and they'd set up lunch."

"Daddy doesn't set up lunch with just anybody," Melissa said. "There are millions of actors who'd kill to have Daddy set up lunch with them. Your father should be very excited."

"Have you heard from your father?" Katie asked. "I bet you're worried about him."

April flashed a look of pure gratitude at her. "Kind of," she said. "He radioed the network last night, and they called us to say everything was okay. There are lots of reporters all around, and search parties, and they think they have some idea of where the plane went down, but they haven't been able to get there yet, and they can't be sure that's the right place until they do. Mom says she'll feel better when Daddy gets back to Nairobi."

"I thought they were divorced," Annabelle declared. "That was what somebody told me."

It was strange to think people were gossiping about her parents. "They are divorced," April said. "But they still worry about each other."

"My mother worries about the support check," Maggie Loomis said. "She says Dad could die for all she cares, just as long as the insurance stays in her name."

"All divorced parents are like that," Annabelle said.

"April's aren't," Katie said. "They still worry about each other."

"Daddy says divorce is what's killing Broadway," Megan said. Sitting across from them gave April a great view of their watches. "He says it's all those young second wives. They don't want to go to plays anymore. They want to go to rock concerts, so their husbands take them, and nobody goes to the theater. The first wives can't afford to go by themselves. Daddy says if the divorce rate doesn't go down soon, then it's off to the Poorhouse we go."

"What's the poorhouse?" Maggie asked.

"I think it's a little theater upstate," Melissa replied. "Where all they do are revivals."

Annabelle shuddered. "You mean you'd have to move from West Devon?" she asked.

"Maybe," Megan said. "Of course, Daddy worries all the time."

"He likes to worry," Melissa said. "Is your father like that, April?"

"A worrier?" April asked. "I don't think so."

"I bet he's worried about Lyon Fitzhugh," Annabelle said. "I know my mother is. She watched the news all day yesterday, just in case they found him. That's how come I saw you so often, April. Because my mother kept watching."

"Your father's been married once before, hasn't he, Annabelle?" Megan said.

"Yeah," Annabelle replied. "I've got two half-sisters older than me."

Melissa nodded. "Your parents are what's killing Broadway," she said. "I bet your father went to the theater all the time with his first wife, and now with your mother he goes to Lyon Fitzhugh concerts."

Annabelle blushed. April couldn't believe it. She didn't think people like Annabelle ever blushed. "They did go to a rock concert once," she said. "But Daddy didn't like it at all. He said everybody was thirty years younger than him and they all dressed funny."

"I wonder how Daddy'll like working at the Poorhouse," Megan said.

"Daddy hates revivals," Melissa said.

April giggled. The other girls stared at her.

"I'm sorry," she said. "It just seems funny to me that just because Annabelle's parents went to a rock concert once, Broadway is dead. And the poorhouse isn't a theater. It's a place poor people go to live. And they don't have them anymore, so your father's just kidding when he says that's where he's going to end. My grandfather likes to say it when my grandmother goes out shopping. He says if she spends another dime, they're going to wind up in the poorhouse. So you can stop worrying."

There was a silence at the table, and April worried that she'd said too much. But then Megan and Melissa laughed.

"That's great," Megan said.

"That's wonderful," Melissa said.

"We've been so scared we were going to end up in some small town in the middle of nowhere putting on revivals," Megan said.

"And Daddy hates revivals," Melissa said.

"Now we know we're going to stay here," Megan said.

"No matter how many Lyon Fitzhugh concerts Annabelle's parents go to," Melissa said.

"If there are any more Lyon Fitzhugh concerts," Maggie said, and suddenly the laughter stopped. "Do they think he's dead?" she asked April. "The reporters and the search parties, I mean."

"I don't know," April said. "I don't think they

know. Daddy says the rescue teams are really good though, very professional, and until they find something bad, there's every reason to keep hoping." Her father had said that on the news the night before, so all the girls at the table probably knew as much as she did, but they listened to her respectfully anyway.

"It's so sad if he's dead," Katie declared. "And his wife expecting a baby."

"Derek if it's a boy," Maggie said. "Marjorie if it's a girl."

"Madelyn," Annabelle said. "That's what you said, wasn't it, April? Madelyn."

"Madelyn," April said.

"And your father really calls him Jeffy?" Katie asked. "Right to his face?"

April nodded.

"Wow," Katie said. "I've never met anybody famous in my whole life."

"We meet famous people all the time," Megan said. "But we never call them Jeffy."

"And all they ever call us is the twins," Melissa said. "They say stuff like, 'Here are the twins. Aren't they cute? Hi, twins.' "

April glanced at them. They were wearing identical blue-and-white sailor dresses. "Maybe if you dressed differently, they wouldn't call you that," she said. "You do look awfully twinlike."

"Daddy makes us wear the same clothes," Megan said.

"He can't tell us apart," Melissa said. "He's never been able to."

"I think it would be easier if you dressed differently," April said. "That way Megan would be the one in red, and Melissa the one in blue."

Megan shook her head. "He says he's too busy to have to learn each morning what we're wearing, and then remember it at night when he gets home."

"Besides, what if we're already in our pajamas when he gets home?" Melissa said. "Lots of nights he gets home really late and we're just about ready for bed. Then even if he's spent all day saying, 'Megan's in red, and Melissa's in blue,' it won't do him any good."

"This way, when we wear the same clothes, he expects to be confused," Megan said. "So he doesn't feel so guilty."

"Daddy hates feeling guilty," Melissa said. "It makes him all sad."

"So we wear the same clothes and he feels better," Megan said. "We love Daddy and he loves us."

April was very glad her family could always recognize her. She looked down at her plate and noticed she'd hardly touched her lunch, and there wasn't that much time left. She began eating as fast as she could.

"My father says it's great you want to be a doctor when you grow up," Katie declared. "He says anytime you want to come over for supper and talk to him about medical schools, he'd be happy to see you."

"Thank you," April said. She hadn't thought about curing anything since Saturday, but she'd been too busy worrying about Lyon Fitzhugh and answering the phone to think about much of anything. "That's very nice of him."

"You really want to be a doctor?" Annabelle asked.

"Maybe," April said. "I haven't decided yet."

"April's mother is a doctor," Megan said.

"No she isn't," April said. "She's a nurse practitioner."

"Well, that's practically the same thing," Megan said.

"No it isn't," April and Katie said simultaneously. They both laughed.

"It's just as good as being a doctor," Katie said. "Only different."

The bell rang for the next class. "Come walk with me," Annabelle said, taking April by the arm. So April did. And once again she was greeted by girls calling her, asking her about Lyon Fitzhugh, telling her they'd seen her on TV, or her father, or both. Annabelle seemed a lot more excited about it than April.

April had planned at the end of the day to see Brooke and give her the Jennifer March interview, but she found she wanted to get home, away from all those strange girls who were now her best friends. So she grabbed her things from her locker and ran home. As she left the school grounds, girls continued to call out to her, but she ignored them. She didn't care what they thought of her. All their attention was giving her a headache.

None of the girls who went to Fairfield lived in her neighborhood, so once she'd made her getaway, April was safe. It was a beautiful September day, the flowers were still in bloom, a few of the trees were starting to change color, and if April hadn't been so worried about Lyon Fitzhugh, and so confused about what had happened in school that day, she would have been very happy indeed.

There were sounds coming from Darcy's apartment, but April decided to check in there anyway. Maybe they'd heard something about Lyon Fitzhugh.

Darcy was sitting in her living room with a couple of her friends. The TV was on to the Continual News Network.

"Any word?" April asked.

"Nothing," Darcy said. "They're still searching. I saw a glimpse of your father, though. They had a story about all the reporters who were there, and they showed your father. They said how Lyon Fitzhugh had spent his last night in Nairobi with him, but they didn't show you after that."

"Good," April said. "I bet all America was getting pretty sick of seeing that interview."

"My mother and I saw it," one of Darcy's friends

said. "And my mother made out a check right away for famine relief."

April smiled. "Really?" she said.

"I bet lots of people had the same reaction," Darcy said. "I bet the famine-relief offices are just being flooded with checks because of your interview."

"All I did was say what Lyon Fitzhugh said to me," April pointed out.

"But you remembered it," Darcy said. "And you told all America about it."

"All America with cable at least," Darcy's other friend said. "Was it exciting being on TV?"

"Darcy says your father knows Lyon Fitzhugh really well," the first girl said. "What's he like?"

"Darcy can tell you as much as I can," April said.

"But you're the one who actually spoke to him," Darcy's friend said. "We want to hear it from you."

April could hear music coming from Isabelle's room. "I have a headache," she said. "I'm going upstairs. Sorry." She tried to smile at Darcy and her friends, then ran from the apartment to her own.

Once she got there, she closed the door, dropped her books, and went to the phone. She dialed Darcy's number, and when Darcy answered the phone, April pinched her nose with her fingers and asked for Isabelle.

"Isabelle!" she heard Darcy call. "It's for you. . . . I don't know. Someone with a cold."

"Hello?" Isabelle said.

"Hi, Isabelle. It's me, April," April said. "I didn't want Darcy to know I was calling."

"All right," Isabelle said. "What can I do for you?"

"I really need to talk to someone," April said. "Could you come up and talk with me?"

April could hear Isabelle take a deep breath. "Sure," she said. "I'll go right now."

"Thank you," April said. She got off the phone and stared at the TV set. Who would have thought being famous could leave such a bad taste in your mouth?

NINE

I'm going out now!" Isabelle called from downstairs, and April could hear her leave the apartment and slam the front door. For a moment she was puzzled, but then Isabelle showed up at the upstairs-apartment door. She was holding her shoes in her hands and tiptoeing.

April opened and closed the door as quietly as she could. "Thanks for coming," she whispered.

"That was fun," Isabelle said in a conversational voice once she was safely in the living room. "I just wish my parents had been home too. I'd love to practice sneaking out on them."

"You didn't sneak out," April said. "You sneaked up."

Isabelle sighed. "You're right," she said. "Oh, well. There goes my career as a delinquent. Now what can I do for you?"

"I don't know," April admitted. "I don't know if anything can be done. I'm just confused."

"Sounds reasonable," Isabelle declared, spreading out on the living-room sofa. "Do you have anything to drink?"

"Only healthy stuff," April replied.

"Oh, yeah," Isabelle said. "I forgot. I should have brought my own junk with me when I sneaked up. Now what's Darcy done to you this time?"

"Nothing," April said. "Why do you say that?"

"Because you wanted me to be so secretive," Isabelle replied. "Tiptoeing and everything."

April didn't think she'd requested tiptoeing, but otherwise Isabelle had a point. "It isn't so much Darcy as it is life," she said. "I'm totally confused, and I needed someone to talk to, and I just didn't want to talk to my mother. You know how mothers are. They worry when you talk to them. They ask you all kinds of mother questions, and then they say it's nothing and you'll outgrow it and they had a problem just like that when they were your age and it turned out to be nothing."

"What's worse is when they tell you about the problem," Isabelle declared. "And not only was it nothing, it was nothing like your problem."

April nodded. "And I can't talk to Darcy because, well, frankly, when I try to talk to her, she ends up doing all the talking. And she mostly talks about herself."

"She *only* talks about herself," Isabelle replied. "Darcy's a one-topic kind of person."

"And I can't talk to Daddy because he's searching for Lyon Fitzhugh," April said. "And I can't talk to any of my friends here, because I don't think I have any. That's what I'm so confused about."

"So I'm fifth choice," Isabelle said. "I'm not offended. You'd be about fifth choice for me, too."

"I just figured you were so poetic and all, you might not know that much about life," April said.

"I know more than you do," Isabelle replied. "I certainly know more than Darcy. And it takes a lot to offend me, so you might as well go on."

Suddenly April's mouth went dry. She had never really talked to Isabelle, who was four years older, and seemed very mature. "I'm going to get some juice," she said. "Would you like some?"

"For lack of anything else, sure," Isabelle said.

April went into the kitchen and poured two glasses. She brought Isabelle one, and then sat down on the rocking chair and sipped from her own. "It's about friends," she said. "Or maybe it isn't. That's what confuses me."

"Start at the beginning," Isabelle said. "You know, juice isn't so bad when you don't surround it with breakfast."

"The beginning," April said. "Before I started school, I didn't have any friends, and Darcy had lots of friends, and she'd invite me to hang around with them, and I'd try, but I never felt comfortable, because they were Darcy's friends and a couple of them acted like they kind of resented me. One of them even called me a rich kid, and we're not rich."

Isabelle nodded. "A lot of kids at the public school resent the Fairfield kids," she said. "And they assume everybody who goes there is rich. Which one of Darcy's friends said that? They can all be pretty dopey."

"I don't remember," April said, although she certainly did. "Anyway, that's not the point. The point is I didn't want to be friends with Darcy's friends, because they'd be Darcy's friends and not mine, and then I started at Fairfield and I brought my friends home—well, they weren't my real friends, but they were girls I wanted to be friends with—and the next thing I know they're visiting Darcy, and they don't even remember I exist. It isn't fair. I keep my hands off her friends when she has so many, and she just steals my friends when I don't have any."

"That rhymes," Isabelle said. "I personally don't write poetry that rhymes, but you might try it."

April had a horrible feeling Isabelle wasn't the right person to talk to either. She was running out of candidates.

Isabelle drank some more of her juice. "Sorry," she said. "About that rhyming business. When you're a poet surrounded by video freaks, you tend to pick up on anything poetic. Including unintentional rhymes."

"Why does Darcy do it?" April asked. "Steal friends, I mean."

"She doesn't," Isabelle said. "Not really. I mean, 'stealing' sounds like she intends to do it, like she goes into the Friendship Store with a gun and steals a batch of them. She's more like a magnet. She attracts friends, and she doesn't care whose friends they are."

"Shouldn't she?" April asked. "I wouldn't magnet her friends, even if she told me to."

Isabelle nodded. "I think it's more who Darcy is than anything else," she said. "Mail carriers love her. Grocery-store cashiers. You should see her at Video To Go. Everybody talks to her. The mayor comes in, she talks; the school principal comes in, he talks. Priests, babies, everybody talks to Darcy."

"Why?" April asked.

"I'm not positive," Isabelle replied. "I think partly she just has the kind of face you talk to. I'd talk to her if she wasn't my sister. And partly Darcy listens. She really does, and she asks all kinds of questions, and she remembers everything. So people think she's interested, and they talk even more. Sometimes I don't blame her for talking so much about herself when she gets home. She doesn't have that much of a chance to when she's in public."

"I listen to people," April said. "When they give me the chance to."

"But do you ask them questions?" Isabelle replied. "Do you make them feel like they're the absolute center of the universe?"

"No," April said. "They're not."

Isabelle grinned. "That's the difference," she declared. "Darcy knows they aren't either, but she makes them feel like they are. Sometimes she even does it with me, turns her full focus on me, and I find myself telling her things I never would have told her otherwise. I get so mad at myself after I've done that, because now she knows all kinds of secrets about me I don't want her to know. I think what it is is Darcy's genuinely interested in people. In everybody. And they sense it, so they talk to her, and poof, she has a new friend."

"I'm not like that," April said.

"Neither is Mom," Isabelle said. "I remember I complained to her once about it. It was a couple of years ago, and my friends would come over, and they'd practically insist on playing with Darcy. When she was real little, I could understand it, because she was cute, and we'd dress her up and play house with her, but when she was ten, all she was was a pest, and my friends still liked having her hang around. It drove me crazy. So I complained to Mom, and she said she went through the same thing with Aunt Joanne. She said it really got bad when she'd bring a boyfriend home, and Aunt Joanne would just steal him. Not meaning to, but poof, the boy would start calling her instead, and Mom would lose another boyfriend."

"That's horrible," April said. "I can't picture Mom doing anything that mean."

"That's the whole point," Isabelle said. "It wasn't supposed to be mean. It was just Aunt Joanne was so outgoing, so good with people, that boys naturally liked her. Mom said when she met Dad, she didn't take any chances. She made sure he was in love with her before she introduced him to Aunt Joanne."

April tried to picture her mother stealing boyfriends and breaking people's hearts, and giggled.

"I know," Isabelle said. "It's weird to think they were ever that young. But they were, I guess. Anyway, if I were you, I wouldn't introduce any of my boyfriends to Darcy."

"I'm not going to have any boyfriends, unless Darcy does the introducing," April replied. "I can't meet any at Fairfield."

"Maybe it'll work out that way," Isabelle said. "Darcy'll know dozens of boys—she already does— and she'll let you have the pick of the litter."

April pictured going out with a springer spaniel and giggled some more.

"You seem happier," Isabelle declared. "Have I solved all your problems for you?"

April shook her head. "There's another one, if you don't mind," she said.

"Not at all," Isabelle replied. "Actually, I'm kind of enjoying this. It makes me feel big sisterish without any of the disadvantages. You know, jealousy, fights, angry parents. Keep going."

"All right," April said, glad to have someone finally paying attention to her. "The girls at Fairfield. They may have liked Darcy right away, but they didn't like me. At least not like that. They didn't hate me or anything, but they didn't care if I was around or not."

Isabelle nodded.

"And then Lyon Fitzhugh disappeared, and Daddy was on TV," April said.

"More to the point, you were on TV," Isabelle declared. "Every hour on the hour."

"Yeah, that too," April said. "And now they want to have lunch with me and they keep inviting me over for dinner, and Megan and Melissa's father wants to put Daddy in a play so he can save Broadway from second marriages."

"What?" Isabelle asked.

"I have trouble with that one too," April said. "But they seemed really serious about it."

"What's the problem?" Isabelle asked. "You don't think they'll stay your friends if Uncle Mitch doesn't agree to star on Broadway?"

April shook her head. "I don't think it's right that they should be my friends just because I was on TV," she said. "That isn't liking you for who you are. It's for who you know. I sort of know Lyon Fitzhugh, and now everybody wants to be with me. What if I didn't? Where would they all be then?"

"Probably hanging out with Darcy," Isabelle replied. "All right. Can I ask a couple of questions?"

"Sure," April said.

"Do you like these girls?" Isabelle began.

April thought about it. "I like Katie," she said. "And the twins are weird, but interesting. I've never known anybody that strange, let alone two of them, if you know what I mean."

"I know exactly what you mean," Isabelle said. "How about the other girls who've been making a fuss over you. You like any of them?"

"I like Emily," April said. "She writes poetry too. But she hasn't made a fuss over me. Maybe that's why I like her. It isn't that I don't like the other girls; it's just I feel like they're phonies for pretending to like me just because I've been famous for a day or two."

"You're right," Isabelle said. "This is complicated. Do you want the kind of advice your mother would give, or at least my mother would, or do you want my honest opinion?"

"Go with honest," April said. "If I wanted mother advice, I could ask my own mother."

"Or mine," Isabelle declared. "She loves giving advice. Let me start with a question."

April giggled. "Like Darcy," she said.

"I should hope not," Isabelle said. "The twins. Why did you like them at first?"

April thought about it. "I guess because they were twins," she said. "The way they look and talk and dress exactly alike."

Isabelle nodded. "Is that who they are or what they are, if you know what I mean?"

"I don't know what you mean," April replied.

"Well, I do," Isabelle said. "What I mean is just because they're twins and they dress the same way and everything, does that make them nice people?"

"No, of course not," April said. "Weird people maybe, but not nice."

"And now that you know them a little better, do you think they're nice?" Isabelle asked.

"I'm not sure yet," April said. "They aren't mean, I know that. And they really do love their father. Not the way other kids love their fathers. More the way I love mine, I think. You know. When you don't see that much of your father, you love him differently."

Isabelle stared at April. "You're smarter than Darcy," she declared. "Did you know that?"

"Kind of," April said. "Darcy sees everything, but sometimes I think she doesn't notice stuff."

"Darcy wouldn't notice a mountain if it landed on her head," Isabelle declared. "But that's beside the point. The problem is, I've forgotten what my point was."

"Maybe I know it," April said. "Maybe the point is I liked the twins before I got to know them just because they were so different, and now I'm mad because they like me when they don't know me because I've been on TV."

Isabelle nodded. "Good point," she said. "I might have put it a bit more poetically, but that's the basic idea."

"So it's okay to be friends with people just because I've been on TV," April said. "You're right. Mom would never tell me that."

"That isn't quite it," Isabelle replied. "It's more like people want to know other people for lots of different reasons, because they're twins, or they have red hair, or a nice laugh, or a way of making you feel important, or because they've been on TV, and that's how friendships start. If you end up not liking someone, you're never going to like them just because they have red hair or they've been on TV. It's just kind of an introduction. This is Jane who has a nice laugh. This is April who's been on TV."

"So being on TV is like having red hair," April said. "It just makes me interesting to people."

Isabelle nodded. "And then after they get to know you, and you get to know them, you become friends," she said. "Or you don't. They may decide that you were on TV, but you're not really very interesting. Or you may decide she has a nice laugh, but she can be really nasty. So you become friends with somebody else."

"Then it's okay," April said, "when girls who never paid attention to me want to have lunch with me and everything?"

"You have to use it," Isabelle said. "It's an opportunity and you have to use it. Like when I see a beautiful sunset. I can see it and admire it and forget about it, or I can see it and write a poem, and then I've used it. You can be April who takes a long time making friends and is on TV, or you can be April who's on TV and uses it to get to know the other girls and see who you want to be friends with. See what I mean?"

"I do," April said. "Thank you. You know, Isabelle, you are kind of like having a big sister without all the problems."

Isabelle grinned. "You know the best part?" she said.

"No, what?"

"Darcy'll never know!"

And the cousins shared a conspiratorial giggle.

TEN

*I*n spite of her talk with Isabelle, April had a miserable night's sleep. She woke up three times from having dreams about Lyon Fitzhugh. In one, he was dead, in another alive, in the third still missing. None of the dreams comforted her.

"Do you think dreams come true?" she asked her mother over breakfast.

"Not often," her mother replied. "Why? Has one of yours?"

April described each dream to her.

Her mother put down her juice glass. "It sounds like one of them is bound to come true," she said. "That's called hedging your bets."

April glanced at the clock and saw it was seven thirty. "May I turn on the radio to the news?" she asked. "Just in case they found him overnight?"

April's mother hated noise first thing in the

morning, but she nodded. "Very softly," she said. "That's all I ask."

April turned the radio on so softly she could barely hear it herself. There was a hurricane in the Bahamas. The Prime Minister of Great Britain met the President. A space launch was scheduled for later that week. And there was no word yet on Lyon Fitzhugh and the people he was traveling with.

"I hope he isn't dead," April said.

"Everyone hopes that," her mother replied.

But April suspected she hoped it more than everyone else. She felt better about her new celebrity, but she was still uncomfortable with the idea that she might have gained it from someone else's death. What if he was dead, and they found his body? Would the Continual News Network run her interview a hundred times more? How would the girls at Fairfield feel about that?

April sighed as she gathered her schoolbooks. Life was easier before she became a star. Not necessarily more pleasant, but definitely easier.

She saw Darcy downstairs, also getting ready for school. The day was warm and sunny, so both girls would be walking. "No word yet," Darcy said. "We watched the news all night until I went to bed, and then I turned it on first thing this morning. Isabelle spent the entire evening in her room writing poetry. She says a little news goes a long way for her, but I really wanted to know."

"Why?" April asked.

"For you," Darcy replied. "I mean, I hope they find Lyon Fitzhugh because he's famous and his wife is pregnant and all that, but I know it's more than that for you, and you must want him to be alive really bad, so I hope he is too. That's all."

April looked at her cousin and smiled. "I love you," she said. She couldn't remember ever having said that to anyone other than her parents before.

Darcy nodded. "I love you too," she said. "But I have to go to school anyway. A great film director needs a solid background in school stuff. At least that's what Mom keeps trying to convince me." She grinned. "I'll see you later," she said.

"After school," April said. She watched as Darcy began her walk, and then she started off on her own. The closer she got to Fairfield, the more girls she saw that she knew. Several of them said hello to her, and she smiled and said hello right back. Katie and the twins actually seemed to be waiting for her. April joined them, and they walked into the school building together. No matter what the cause, April felt more at home than she had in months.

She tried hard to concentrate on her class work that morning, but it wasn't easy. She knew that daydreaming wasn't going to bring Lyon Fitzhugh back, but that didn't seem to matter. It seemed almost foolish to study French and math when there was a whole world out there with important things going on. April knew her father spoke French along with all his other languages, and she suspected he might once have studied math, but what good did that do him covering the news in Africa? In a famine or a revolution, did it matter that the reporters knew how to determine a square root?

April pictured herself a real reporter, not the Jennifer March kind who covered spelling bees, but one more like her father, a reporter who got dirty from her work. Not in Africa though. Maybe she could cover crime stories. Darcy would love that. Once April had found out all the facts, Darcy could turn them into movies.

The class was trying to determine the square root of 2,014. April sighed, and began to pay attention. She was sure it would turn out to be a perfectly fascinating number.

But before she had the chance to find out, a girl came into the classroom, walked over to Mrs. King, their teacher, and whispered something. Mrs. King nodded.

"There's a phone call for April," she said. "April, you may go to the main office to take the call."

All the other girls turned to face April. Mostly they looked interested, but Katie seemed worried. April wasn't sure what to feel.

"You'd better take your books," Mrs. King said. "The period's almost over."

April nodded. She collected her books, then followed the other girl to the office. April had never gotten a call in school before. She tried to remember if she'd ever been in a class when another kid got a call, and one came back to her. Two years before, David Deal. They called him because his mother had just had a baby. It seemed unlikely to April that her call was about that. Her mother had seemed very unpregnant that morning.

"Do you know who's calling?" she asked the girl.

The girl shook her head. "I was just in the office waiting to speak to Dr. Foster," she said. "And then the phone call came and they sent me to get you."

April nodded. Dr. Foster was headmistress of the school. "Did anybody cry?" she asked. "Like it was bad news for me?"

"Nobody did anything," the girl said. "I sure hope I get to see Dr. Foster right away. Otherwise I'll miss lunch."

April realized she was hungry. She hoped it wasn't bad news, because then she'd feel she shouldn't eat, and she'd just end up miserable and hungry. She walked a little faster then, to get the suspense over with.

They were waiting for her at the office. "It's your mother," the school secretary said, handing April the phone.

"April, honey, I hope I didn't scare you," her mother's reassuring voice said. "It's good news."

"What?" April asked. For a moment she got

confused, and thought her mother was going to announce the birth of a baby. She realized then just how hungry she was.

"I just heard from your father," her mother said. "It should be on the radio soon. They found the plane, and Lyon Fitzhugh is all right. Everyone is. It was a miracle. The plane went down, and a couple of people were hurt slightly, nothing serious, and they just waited to be rescued. They didn't have many supplies with them, but apparently Jeffy, I mean Lyon, said it was good that they were hungry and scared. It made them want to fight even more for the people in the camps, because they'd had a little taste of their terror. Mitch said Lyon was amazing, completely in control of the situation. He gave Mitch a ten-minute exclusive interview about the crash, and the network is going to run the whole thing on the news tonight. April? Are you still there?"

"I sure am, Mom," April said. "That's great. I'm just trying to understand it all."

"So's everyone else," her mother said. "Mitch said reporters were actually crying, they were so thrilled no one had died."

"And it isn't a secret?" April asked. "Everyone can know?"

"They will soon enough," her mother said. "Mitch said he knew you must be worrying, and that was why he called me right after he spoke to the network. It may even be on the radio already."

"Thanks, Mom," April said. "Did Daddy say when he'd call again?"

"After he gets back to Nairobi," her mother replied. "We'll watch him on the news tonight, and that'll have to do for the next few days. He's going on with the Fitzhugh party to the camps, first."

"We'll have to tape him," April said.

"We'll have every VCR in the house going," her mother said. "Now get back to class before you miss anything important. I'll see you this afternoon."

"Right, Mom," April said. "And thanks."

"I love you, honey," her mother said, and hung up.

April looked at the school secretary. "May I make a call?" she asked.

The secretary nodded.

April dug through her assignment pad until she found the number she needed. She dialed it, listened to it ring twice, and then said, "Jennifer March, please."

It took another half minute before Jennifer March got on the phone. "Jennifer March," she said. "Who's calling?"

"April Hughes," April said. "Remember? We interviewed each other last week."

"Of course I remember," Jennifer said. "What can I do for you, April?"

"I thought you'd want to know they found Lyon Fitzhugh," April said. "My mother just called to tell me. My father called her, and he was there, so that's how I know. He's all right. Lyon Fitzhugh, I mean. Everyone on the plane is. They still plan to go to the camps, so they must be."

"That's wonderful," Jennifer said. "Could you come over after school today, so I can interview you again for Channel Six?"

"I guess so," April said.

"Write down everything your mother told you," Jennifer March said, "while it's still fresh in your mind. And I'll see you at three thirty."

"Okay," April said. She didn't feel any need to write things down since she was sure she'd remember every word her mother said for the rest of her life. But she scribbled the most important things anyway, so if Jennifer March asked to see her notes, she'd have something to show.

By the time she got to the lunchroom, everyone was eating. She noticed there was an empty chair between Katie and Melissa, and with a start she realized they were holding it for her. April walked over to the chair, put her books down, and smiled.

"What was it?" Katie asked. "Is everybody okay?"

"Fine," April said. "How do you make announcements around here?"

"You just do," Megan said. "Go to the front of the room and shout for attention. Why? What do you have to announce?"

"You'll see," April said. She couldn't believe her nerve. She walked to where Megan had pointed and clapped her hands a couple of times over her head real loudly to get everyone's attention.

The other girls stared at her. April couldn't blame them.

"I have an announcement to make!" she shouted, and then as the room grew silent, she realized she didn't have to shout at all. "I'm April Hughes, and my father is Mitchell Hughes, the Africa correspondent for DBC News, and he just called my mother, she lives here in West Devon, and he told her they found the plane that Lyon Fitzhugh was on, and everybody's all right. Nobody died or anything."

The room fell quiet again, and then all the girls began cheering and applauding. Even the teachers were clapping.

April waited until the noise died down. "My father said everyone was okay," she continued. "A couple of minor injuries, but that was it. And Lyon Fitzhugh plans to keep on with his fight against famine. He said they were hungry there, and scared, and that the hunger and fear made them all the more determined to fight against hunger elsewhere."

The girls continued to listen. It was a funny feeling, knowing that every single person in that room was focused on her, on what she had to say. Days before, they hadn't known she existed, and now she was the center of their attention. She would have been scared, but she knew what she was about to say was important.

"So it seemed to me if Lyon Fitzhugh, who's such a big star and his wife is going to have a baby, and he's been missing in a plane crash for days now, if the first thing he says is he's going to fight against world hunger, then maybe we should do something too," April said. "At Fairfield. Not go hungry, but couldn't we raise money for Ethiopian relief funds? I don't know how you, how we, do that kind of thing, since I'm new here, but it seemed like a good idea."

"It's a great idea!" one of the girls called, and then they were all applauding again.

April stood still and watched as the room went wild. She decided then she wasn't going to be a crime reporter. She'd be a politician instead, or maybe a fund-raiser. It didn't matter which, just as long as she could use her power to help other people.

ℰLEVEN

April stood nervously as Brooke and Mrs. Holcomb read copies of her interview with Jennifer March. She'd finally finished it the night before. Somehow everything was easier to do once she'd learned Lyon Fitzhugh was all right.

She'd thought about showing the piece to her family, the way she had her Lyon Fitzhugh interview, but then she decided against it. Not even her mother got to read it. This is what journalism is all about, she told herself as she shifted her weight from one foot to the other. Just the reporter and the editors. No mothers, aunts, uncles, or cousins allowed.

"What flood?" Brooke asked, breaking the silence.

"What do you mean, what flood?" April asked right back.

"You say here, 'Jennifer March remembered Mrs. Holcomb very well, saying she had been the teacher-advisor on the *Fairfield Forward* since before the West Devon flood.' I don't remember any flood in West Devon."

"Neither do I," Mrs. Holcomb said. "Is that a direct quote, April?"

April checked her notes. "She said you'd been the advisor since before the flood," she replied. "So I guessed it must have been a flood here. We just moved here, so I don't know much West Devon history yet."

Mrs. Holcomb laughed. "It's an expression, April," she said. "It refers to Noah and his ark. It means I've been around forever."

April blushed.

"I think we can just reword that sentence," Mrs. Holcomb said, "so it's clear that Jennifer remembers me, without suggesting that I predate the American Revolution."

"I'm sorry," April said.

"No need for you to apologize," Mrs. Holcomb replied. "Jennifer's the one who said it."

Still, April felt badly as Mrs. Holcomb and Brooke resumed reading. The Jennifer March interview was her first important piece, and already it had problems. The last thing April intended to do was insult Mrs. Holcomb.

"Oh, my," Mrs. Holcomb said when she'd finished reading. "I'm afraid you're going to have to do a lot of rewriting, April."

"Why?" April asked. She was reasonably sure she'd spelled everything correctly, and her grammar was all right. Everything else was simply what Jennifer March had said.

Mrs. Holcomb smiled at April. "I should have had you read some of our alumna-interview pieces first," she said. "So you could get an idea of exactly what we wanted."

"Didn't you want an interview?" April asked. "I'm sorry about that flood mistake, but except for that, I quoted Jennifer March completely accurately." She held up her notepad as evidence.

"I'm sure you did," Mrs. Holcomb replied. "That's the problem."

"I like it," Brooke declared.

Mrs. Holcomb stared at her.

"I do," she said. "It's honest. So what if Jennifer comes off like a fool? All April did was quote."

"We can't have things like this in the *Forward*," Mrs. Holcomb said. " 'I don't get a lot of respect here, at Channel Six. I'm new, and my uncle owns the station. . . .' Or 'My father's a bank president, my uncle's a judge, so it wouldn't be right for me to investigate them.' Or 'Basically my family's boring. . . . It's no trick to own a town the size of West Devon.' Or 'I'd rather my uncle owned DBC than Channel Six. I'd get ahead a lot faster that way.' Or

'A school like Fairfield, a town like West Devon, they manufacture complacent people.' We simply can't, Brooke."

"But if that's what she said—" Brooke protested.

"We either rewrite this piece substantially, or we don't publish it at all," Mrs. Holcomb declared. "I'm sorry, girls, but that's the way it is."

"The alumna interviews are always exactly the same," Brooke said. "I can recite them by heart. We find someone and she goes on about how she got her foundation for living from Fairfield and it taught her how to be a team player and now she's married and has two beautiful children and her husband's president or CEO of this corporation or that and she does volunteer work twice a week at the hospital. Why do you think no one reads them? They're identical and they're boring, and now we have one that's different and interesting, and you say we can't print it?"

"That's exactly what I say," Mrs. Holcomb replied.

"I didn't make up any of those quotes," April said. "Honest."

Mrs. Holcomb smiled at her. "I'm sure you didn't," she replied. "The problem is we sent our youngest interviewer to our youngest alumna, and frankly, they both come off sounding too young."

"Better young than mother of two beautiful children," Brooke grumbled.

"We could publish April's piece exactly as is,"

Mrs. Holcomb said. "And we would make a lot of parents angry. Dr. Foster would also be angry. The alumnae who receive copies of the *Forward* would be angry as well. But the person who would be most hurt would be Jennifer March, when she saw how foolish she sounded. And I won't have her hurt that way. I like her too much."

"But she said every one of those things," Brooke said. April was pleased, and a little surprised, that Brooke was fighting on her side.

Mrs. Holcomb nodded. "I'm sure she did. But let me tell you something. Some day, a few years from now, you'll both say something to someone about yourselves, about your lives, and as soon as you say it, you'll think, 'Thank God nobody I know will ever read that.' You'll have been a little too honest, or unguarded, and what should be an innocent comment will come out hurtful or simply foolish. And you'll remember us here today, and all those things Jennifer said that she shouldn't have, and you'll understand why I won't print the piece."

"How many years will I have to wait?" Brooke asked.

Mrs. Holcomb laughed. "Fewer than you think," she said.

"Does this mean I can't write for the *Forward* anymore?" April asked.

"Absolutely not," Mrs. Holcomb said. "You have that piece about Lyon Fitzhugh. I think another one about being interviewed by Jennifer

March, and then being on national TV, would make for wonderful reading. What do you think, Brooke?"

Brooke pursed her lips, then nodded. "Be honest," she said. "Just not too honest."

"Write up the whole story," Mrs. Holcomb suggested. "From your interview with Lyon until yesterday's call saying he was all right. Say you met Jennifer for a possible alumna interview. That way no one will wonder where the interview went."

"What are we going to do about the alumna interview?" Brooke asked. "We have one every issue."

"Someone can interview me," Mrs. Holcomb said. "I'm an alumna, you know. I went to Fairfield sometime before the Flood."

"I hope you'll give me another chance," April said. "To write about something other than me and Lyon Fitzhugh, I mean."

"We will," Brooke said. "I think you have a real future here at the *Forward*, April."

April stared at her.

"I really do," Brooke said. "First I thought you were just some young kid who didn't know what to do, and then I thought you were a little full of yourself, not to mention lucky, but now I think you really have potential. I like your interview with Jennifer March. I think next issue we'll send you to interview someone else, who'll maybe open up just a little more than she otherwise would."

"Brooke," Mrs. Holcomb said.

"Not too much more," Brooke said. "Just a little."

"My cousin Darcy goes to the Middle School," April said. "And her friends don't seem to much like me because I go to Fairfield. I thought maybe I could interview them, and some of the other kids, and find out what they think about Fairfield students. We live in the same town. I think we should know what they think of us."

"That sounds great," Brooke said.

"It's certainly worth trying," Mrs. Holcomb said. "I can see you're going to be an interesting person to work with, April."

"I'll try," April said. "Thank you. Should I take the Jennifer March interview, or do you want to keep it?"

"I need a copy," Mrs. Holcomb said. "I'm going to call Jennifer and give her a little talk about learning to think before she speaks. She's old enough to hear it."

"How about getting together with me next week?" Brooke said to April. "We can work out some questions for you to ask the Middle School kids."

"Great," April said, smiling at both of them. She had never known rejections could be so painless. She took her books and left the classroom.

"How'd it go?" Katie asked in the hallway.

"You were waiting for me?" April asked.

Katie nodded. "Megan and Melissa wanted to, but they had to go to New York to have supper with their father," she said. "They said to tell you next time they go in, they want you to go with them so their father can meet you. My parents want to meet you too. My father says you must be even more compassionate than he thought, because you suggested that famine-relief fund from Fairfield, and he thinks you'd make a really great doctor. Anyway, I waited. How'd it go?"

"They turned my interview down," April said. "But I got another assignment, so I guess it's okay."

"I'd die if they turned me down," Katie said. "You don't even look like you cried."

"I blushed a lot," April admitted. "But Mrs. Holcomb really is nice. And Brooke was on my side. So there wasn't much point crying."

"I still think you're tough and brave," Katie declared. "As well as compassionate."

"Isn't that Emily over there?" April asked.

Katie nodded. "I guess she stayed late today too," she said.

"I wish I knew her better," April said.

"Emily's shy," Katie said. "She started school here last year and she still hasn't made any real friends."

"I'm going to talk to her," April said, and walked over to Emily. Katie followed her. "Hi, Emily," she said. "How's your poetry?"

Emily stared at her. "How did you know I write poetry?" she asked.

"You mentioned it at that *Forward* meeting," April replied. "And I remembered, because my cousin Isabelle writes poetry too. Would you like to meet her?"

"I guess," Emily said. "Where does she live?"

April laughed. "About half a mile from here," she said. "We live in a two-family house together. She's downstairs, with my other cousin, Darcy, and I'm upstairs. We have parents there too."

"Darcy's funny," Katie said. "She's going to be a great film director."

"How does she know?" Emily asked. "Maybe she'll only be a very good film director."

"Don't say that to Darcy," April said with a laugh. "Are you free now? Would you like to come home with me and meet them and talk to Isabelle about poetry? I'd like to hear about it too."

"You mean right now?" Emily asked.

April nodded. "You're invited too, Katie," she said.

"Great," Katie said. "Come on, Emily. It'll be fun."

Emily smiled at them. "I'll have to call Mrs. Coombs when I get there," she said. "She's our housekeeper, and she needs to know where I am."

"No problem," April said. "We have a phone."

"I know," Emily said. "Well, you spoke to Lyon Fitzhugh on one."

April laughed. The girls gathered their things and left the school building together. The sun shone down on them as they walked the ten blocks.

"I didn't know you just started at Fairfield last year," April said to Emily. "Where did you live before?"

"In Rome," Emily said.

"Rome as in Italy?" April asked.

Emily nodded.

"That's great," April said. "I used to live in Madrid. I didn't think anybody in West Devon ever lived anyplace interesting before."

"That's not fair," Katie said. "I used to live someplace interesting too."

"Where?" April asked.

"Chicago," Katie said. "I was born there. Of course we moved to West Devon when I was one, but even so, I lived in Chicago."

"Before we lived in Rome, we lived in Tokyo," Emily said. "But I was only four when we moved to Rome."

"Do you speak any Italian?" April asked.

"Sure," Emily said. "Do you speak Spanish?"

April nodded.

"I speak English," Katie said. "That's what they speak in Chicago, you know."

The girls laughed.

128

"It's hard going to a new school," Emily said. "I've kind of been watching you, April, and you make it seem so easy, making friends, and making announcements to the whole school, and writing for the *Forward* and everything."

"None of it's been easy," April replied. "Katie's helped me a lot."

"I have?" Katie said. "I didn't know that."

"That's because you're compassionate too," April said. "You'd be a great doctor yourself if you ever got over your fear of gallbladders."

"I'm not afraid of gallbladders," Katie said. "I just don't want to eat one."

"Eat a gallbladder," Emily said. "Yuck."

"Yuck and a half," April said. "There's our house up ahead."

"It's so pretty," Emily said. "The house we live in is all modern and boring. I love all this trim work."

"It's called gingerbread," April said. She unlocked her front door. "Darcy! Isabelle! Are either of you home?"

"We both are," Darcy said, opening the door to her apartment. "Hi, April. Hi, Katie."

"This is Emily," April said. "She writes poetry and she used to live in Rome."

"Rome, Italy?" Darcy asked.

Emily nodded.

"Lots of great film directors live there," Darcy said. "I'm going to be one someday, but I don't think I'll live in Rome. Hey, Isabelle. There's someone here for you to meet. Do you want to come on in?"

"We'll be up in my room," April said. "Why don't you come there?"

"Sure," Darcy said. "We'll be up in a couple of minutes."

"And bring cookies and sodas," April said. "I have a wonderful mother, but she hates junk food," she told her friends.

"Next time we'll have to come to my house," Emily said. "Mrs. Coombs bakes all the time."

"Mrs. Dorman—that's our housekeeper—she sticks to store-bought," Katie declared. "She says my parents don't pay her enough to make her bake."

"Knock knock," Darcy said, since the door to April's apartment was wide open. "Can we come in?"

April said yes, and soon her apartment was filled with the sound of Italian and Spanish and laughter and poetry and cousins and chocolate-chip cookies.

Susan Beth Pfeffer, who has *lots* of noisy cousins, lives in Middletown, New York. She is the author of many popular books for young readers, among them *The Year Without Michael* and *Dear Dad, Love, Laurie.*